Omega and the Witch

A book in the Sanctuary Series

Book Two

J. Raven Wilde

Copyright

Published by Twisted Crow Press, LLC

www.twistedcrowpress.com

ISBN: 979-8-9906871-5-8

Other Books by J. Raven Wilde

Standalone Novels

His Orders

Hot and Steamy Series

In Hot Pursuit

Hot Rod

One Hot Weekend

Falling For Series

Falling for the Rancher

Falling for the Cowboy

The Mummy's Curse Mini-Series

The Mummy's Curse Vol 1

The Sorcerer's Curse Vol 2

The Curse of Anubis Vol 3

The Mummy's Curse Mini-Series Box Set

Sanctuary Series

Claimed by the Alpha

The Omega and the Witch

The Rogue and the Rebel

Deerskin Peaks Series

Claimed by the Bear

Taming the Wildcat

I want to thank all my readers for your patience in waiting for Omega and the Witch to come out. This book has been long overdue. I had been dealing with health issues, mental and physical, and had been dealing with a toxic relationship for a lot longer than I should have among other things. I am happy to be writing again and am overly joyed to be able to finish John's story and get it out to you.

This book was originally published a chapter at a time on Amazon Kindle Vella. This ebook is the most current and updated version.

1

Aiden

As I picked up my phone sitting on the desk in my office, I drew in a deep breath, released it in a deep sigh, and cleared my throat as I prepared to make a very important phone call. It had been a while since I had to call the Council with less-than-great news. I've taken a few lives in my lifetime. Some, as pack master, but it was the first time I had taken another alpha's life after he challenged me.

Gemma was my mate, and I was going to protect her even if her dad, who was an alpha, challenged me. I should've called the Council a lot sooner about what had happened. Instead, I let a few weeks pass by. I figured that once I explained the details of the incident, all would be forgiven, including my delay in reporting the events. Not only was I newly mated, but I also had my pack to consider, as most of them were suffering from moon sickness because of me.

"Councilman Richards, I hope you are well," I said in a cheerful tone once he answered the phone. "I am Aiden McKinney, alpha of the Northwest US territory."

"Pack Master Aiden," he drawled in his southern accent. "What do I owe the pleasure of this phone call? I heard rumors that you have finally mated. I'm guessing your rutting season is over and you wished to inform us? Hopefully, you were successful in planting an heir."

"Yes, Councilman Richards. I believe I was very successful."

"That's good to hear," he said cheerfully.

"I also have news of the loss of one of your alphas," I said, wanting to get down to business. "Pack Master Smith from New York. Sadly, he had challenged me, and I had no choice but to accept. I also killed his second-in-command, Foster. Foster had kidnapped my mate and my brother. He had threatened to force himself on her and attacked my second-in-command."

"I see," he said with a sigh.

The tone of his sigh told me that he wasn't pleased, and I was dreading what my punishment would be, if any. Death challenges were becoming fewer and fewer as we updated our laws with the times. My father was the pack master before me, and he handed me the role when he felt he could no longer be the alpha and lead our pack. No challenge was needed, even though that was the way it was done. My father believed in modernization. He wanted to protect the supernatural kind from the human world as much as we could, as our numbers were sorely depleting. Keeping up with the times was one of the best ways to do so.

The Council encouraged modernization for the same reason. However, some of our old ways are still in place as a formality, so I knew I wouldn't be punished severely for what transpired. However, the timing of my report could have landed me in hot water.

"Although I'm not too happy to hear about all of this, I'm honestly not too sorry that it was Smith and Foster who lost their lives. Smith had been quite troublesome for some time now, breaking many of the pack laws and a few human laws, and he began to create problems between us and the human world."

We had given him far too many warnings and were considering replacing him and his officers. Now, you have taken care of him for us. However, I'm sorry to inform you that you cannot take charge of two packs unless they are within the same region. Have you named your successor?"

"I named my brother John as a temporary alpha," I said, even though I was sure he wouldn't be viable to be an alpha.

"Would that be your pack's omega?"

"Yes, sir," I replied. I knew from his question that he was not happy with my choice.

"An omega may not be feasible with this pack. I fear that this pack is far beyond an omega's help at this point. They need a dominant wolf to sort this pack out as they are ruthless and would tear an omega to shreds."

"I will send my third to accompany him for cautionary measures. He's dominant enough to step in should he need to."

"That sounds doable. Be ready to announce their replacements if something goes wrong," Councilman Richards warned. "You must announce a better successor, or one will be made for you."

"I do have another wolf in mind. He's alpha material and would be a great pack master." I didn't plan on having John take over completely. I indeed did have someone else in mind. My cousin Vince. However, I had yet to reach him and convince him that he was, in fact, up for the part of pack master whether he knew it or not.

"We would need him to select his officers immediately and get the pack up to modern traditions. I recommend that his officers aren't part of the original pack to refrain from any setbacks. Is he on his way?"

"I gave him a deadline to decide," I lied. He wasn't going to let me down. He had no choice. Though he decided he wanted to be a rogue wolf, he was still a part of this pack and needed to come back and take up the role placed upon him by his alpha.

"You have three weeks. That's all I can afford you. After that, if you haven't named your successor, we'll have no choice but to name one for you."

"Understood." I didn't have to say anything else as Councilman Richards had hung up on me.

Smith's pack was on the east coast in New York, and mine was on the west coast, in Oregon. I had no intention of taking over their pack. Per law, I couldn't because of geographical location. However, I went out to meet and greet the pack, and Councilman Richards was right; they are an ugly, unruly bunch. I already had a few attempted challenges, but they hadn't followed through. I was still on edge as my mating ritual was cut a little short, and I was still trying to take care of my *own* pack back home. Following through with an actual challenge would prove careless on their part, and they could sense it.

I owed my brother a lot. It was a rough time for my pack and me, and he helped me through it with his gift. Brokenhearted and stubborn, I blamed myself for not being able to protect my pack from what occurred. That was on me. John used all his energy to keep me from being stuck in my wolf form.

He also found Gemma and helped me to see who she truly was. Once we were finally mated, you could feel the relief from the pack as they could finally shift back to their human form. Everyone came around to congratulate me and to thank John for protecting their alpha. Now, our pack bond had strengthened, and we were a strong pack once again.

My only hope was that my brother could help the New York pack. It needed a lot of work, which was why I was sending Paul, my third-in-command. I entrusted him with my life. He didn't argue when I made John my second, even though he had every right to be mad. We had grown up together and even served a few tours in the Army together. He deserved that spot more than anyone else in my pack. I trusted Paul to protect my brother as he would protect me.

Now that the hard part was over, I still had one more thing to do — tell my brother about his new position, followed by making a phone call to my cousin.

John knocked twice before entering my office. "Hey, brother. How did the phone call go?" he asked as he walked over to one of my bookshelves and leaned against it.

I stared at my brother momentarily, trying to find a way to tell him I was sending him to New York to manage an unruly pack in my place.

"It went about as expected," I said coolly.

"From your expression, it looks like they aren't too upset over the loss of an alpha, but something tells me there is more. What is it?"

That's what made my brother's gift incredible. He was very intuitive and could sense things. "I'm sending you to New York to take over as alpha in my place. They're some fairly big shoes to fill, but I know you can do it."

"Massive shoes if you are being serious. Huge shoes." He paused, then cocked an eyebrow once he realized I wasn't joking. "Wait, what? Aiden, you can't be serious. Seems as if I'll be filling clown shoes if you think I can be an alpha."

"Look, you're an omega," I said calmly, trying to make my case.

"Yeah, not an alpha, brother. Their alpha tried to kill me if you remember. So, sending me isn't the best idea. Is that what the Council wanted me to do?"

"Not really, no."

"Not really? So, it's your idea, then?" I could hear the pain in his tone. He was doubting his capabilities.

"Yes, but hear me out."

"This better be a good explanation. Brother, you know I will do anything for you, but that."

John walked over and sat in one of the chairs in front of my desk. The very chair that the alpha I had killed sat in not that long ago. The same alpha whose pack John was supposed to command in my place, however short it would be.

I leaned back in my chair, took a deep breath, and then released it in a loud sigh. "The Council doesn't want you to go. Clearly, they know how ruthless and disorderly this pack ias. However, you're an omega and can at least bring some sort of calm and peace to the pack."

John drew a hand through his hair. "I doubt that would happen. I love you, brother, but I can't do what you're asking me to do."

"I'm not asking you as my brother, but as your alpha."

John shook his head and let out a breathy laugh. "Damn you, Aiden. That's twisting my arm. Are you getting back at me for undermining you in hiring Gemma?"

I leaned back in my chair and gave him a wolfish grin. "In a way, but then I do have to thank you for helping me find my mate."

He rolled his eyes, "Some thanks I'm getting. Those wolves will have my hide, literally." John sighed and said, "Can I take someone with me? You know I'll need someone alpha enough to step in and help when I need it."

"You're doubting your abilities as an Omega, little brother. And, yes, I'm sending Paul with you."

"That's good. He's the best choice to take your spot as alpha, though, not me."

"I'm sure he'll thank you for that, but I need you on this one. The Council wants someone who will relieve you in three weeks."

"Three weeks," he scoffed. "Thank goodness for that. I hope I can last that long."

"You'll do fine, brother. I have faith in you," I said with a small smile.

"I'm not doubting anything. Based on what your mate told us and from your short visit there, I'm simply worried about how unlawful this pack is. Not to mention if the Council doesn't want me to go. Who do you have in mind to take your place?"

"Our cousin Vince."

John let out a loud laugh as if what I said was hilarious. "You have lost your mind." He leaned over the desk with an outreached hand and placed it on my forehead as if he were testing my temperature. "You aren't feverish."

He looked me over as if inspecting me for any underlying illnesses as I swatted his hand away with an annoyed scowl. He was probably checking to see if my lost marbles were tangling from my ears. I believed they had slipped out long before I met with Councilman Richards when I thought about sending my dear brother.

"That alpha must've hit you on the head hard because I know, and you know, and our dear cousin knows he isn't alpha material. He's a rogue, Aiden, if you remember correctly. Lone wolves don't want anything to do with being part of a pack, let alone be an alpha."

"Look, brother. He's the best choice so far. I need you here in *this* pack. You're our omega. You're what keeps us together. If we didn't have you, there's no telling what would've happened to the rest of the pack. To me." John was far too valuable for our pack to lose, but I knew how useful he could be in helping put some peace and order back into a pack. I needed him to do that to the one in New York.

"I know you hated me working behind your back, looking for a mate, but we couldn't let you fall deeper into moon sickness."

"I was close, John. Very close."

"I know, man," he sighed.

"That's why I need you to work your magic on that pack. The Council needs them to start following the rules."

John stood up and released a sigh. "I'll start packing. I'll be sure to give your mate a goodbye kiss." He made it to the door before saying the last part, knowing that would stir me. I couldn't help but laugh.

My mating rutting ritual had been over a few days ago, but I still have the urge to take her to bed every chance I get. Gemma was a treasure that John was lucky to have found. I didn't know it then, but Gemma and John saved me and the rest of the pack.

A few of my pack mates were stuck in their wolf forms because of me. I had lost my wife and child and felt grief-stricken. My wolf surfaced more often than he should have, coming close to taking over. I barely had a handle on my human self, but only with John's help as an omega would he be able to keep me sane just long enough to continue being the pack's alpha.

Not every pack has an omega. They aren't rare. However, only very few exist. They are not only submissive, but they are also the peacekeepers and keep our wolves in check. I trusted John to be able to work his omega magic. I just hoped it was long enough for our cousin to show up and take over. I had a duty to my pack. They needed me more, and I had a duty and obligation to my wife, Gemma, and any potential offspring we may have.

2

John

I didn't want to go to New York. I was happy being on the East Coast, but I understood that my brother, my alpha needed me to take his place. Because I was an Omega, I was able to keep him from falling deeper into moon sickness, but only due to the cost of the pack. He had gone too long without a mate. An alpha without a mate was terrible news for the pack. He starts turning to his wolf more and more. A mate keeps him grounded enough for him to be able to take on his responsibilities and shift without any issues.

I was nervous after talking to Aiden about the pack I was about to visit. Their former alpha was coldblooded and cruel, doing whatever he could to get his daughter back and to use her as a pawn in his own selfish endeavors. Would it benefit his pack? Possibly, but at what costs? Aiden told me that was how that alpha ran the pack.

We've come a long way in improving our laws in how we treat our pack members and our mates, especially females. Our Council had spent many painstaking years trying to rebuild our packs and rewrite our laws. They had to step in on a few occasions to take over when a pack master felt they could not be swayed into following any new laws or when an alpha attempted to break their pack away from the Council, making it their own entity. That would prove dangerous for us and the humans as we tried to hide ourselves from them as best we could.

Aiden and I shared the same father. He was a great alpha to our pack and taught us to respect our pack members, especially our females, and to keep the humans from knowing anything about us. He was a little more challenging when it came to being a father. My father was harder on me when he found out what I was. He wanted his sons to be alpha material. That was why he spent more time with Aiden and gave him his last name, having me take my mother's. Father was coaching Aiden into taking over for him as pack master. I guess, deep down, he wanted two wolves that were dominant enough to lead the pack — when Aiden took his role as alpha, I would be strong enough to be his second. To have such a dynamic would strengthen the pack and help it grow.

When it came time for our father to step down, he was the only one who disagreed with Aiden's choice to make me second-in-command. The Council said it wasn't the best choice, but they would allow it as we needed an omega. Aiden had to choose a more dominant wolf for a third-in-command, though.

I remember when Aiden tried to offer the position to our cousin, Vince, but Vince declined it. Not long after that, Vince told us he wanted to go rogue. Aiden wasn't happy but had no choice in the matter. Aiden told Vince he would still be considered part of the pack and had to check in occasionally.

I hoped Aiden knew what he was doing, choosing Vince as pack master. Vince is a great guy, but I was sure he needed the freedom to come and go whenever he wanted to without worrying about being restrained by rules. I also hoped that Aiden had a backup plan in case Vince declined. A small part of me felt that Aiden hadn't asked him yet because why would my brother be sending me to New York instead of Vince? Or, he did ask and Vince told him he needed some time to think about it.

I didn't want to be in New York longer than I had to. In fact, I prayed that I didn't have to be there for three weeks. I had a feeling I would be. I was fortunate to have Paul with me. He should've been Aiden's choice to step in as pack master for New York. I honestly believed Paul was more of an alpha wolf and a much better choice than Vince.

3

Kara

It was a beautiful summer morning. It was perfect weather for picking herbs in my garden and foraging for the wild herbs that grew around here. Some of my healing oils and ointments were getting low, as were my herbs for cooking, and I needed to stock up, putting some away for the winter. I had a greenhouse for some of those ingredients, but the window of opportunity was closing for the rest I would find out in the wild. I grabbed one of my baskets off my front porch and made my way to the tree line, where I usually found a few goodies.

I had a love/hate relationship with where I lived. My mother stumbled upon this place when she was pregnant with me. The farmer who owned this land was a widower, took a liking to my mother, and let her stay here. When the widower discovered that my mother wanted to help other women like herself, she gifted the cabin and a few acres surrounding it to my mother. With the widower's help, my mother, a powerful witch, had turned this piece of property into a sanctuary for other women.

You see, this place was not too far away from another influential person—a wolf so arrogant and manipulative that my mother loathed him with all her being. Mother had cast powerful wards protecting this place from him and anyone else who wished to cause harm to anyone who crossed the protection boundary of the sanctuary. I loved the beauty of the place. I simply hated my neighbors and the trouble that they created.

The moment I reached the area I was hoping to begin my search, I heard a woman's voice franticly shrieking for help. My heart jumped, and I immediately began to search for this person. I headed in the direction I knew she would be coming from. This wasn't the first time. It had been a while since I had a woman running to me for help. I only wished it was the last.

"Come to my voice," I yelled out. My eyes scanned the area for anyone running through the woods. The trees and brush became denser the further I went, making it hard to see anything past them. "Hey," I shouted again. "I'm here if you can come to me."

Finally, I could see someone approaching me, so I picked up my pace to meet them. A woman who appeared worse for wear and not far along in her pregnancy. It was a blessing she had left when she did.

"Are you Kara?" she asked as she slowed to a moderate walk, breathing heavily.

"I am," I replied. I peered over her shoulder, but I couldn't see anyone. I knew they were there. I could sense them. However, I didn't know how far away they were.

"They're after me," she said. Her words were staggered, telling me she was exhausted. She drew deep breaths through her nose, releasing it through her mouth slowly. A way to get the heart rate to drop and catch her breath.

"I'll take care of them," I said as I closed the distance between us. The moment I reached her, she collapsed in my arms. "I got you, but we have to keep moving."

She shook her head and said, "I'm so tired." She looked defeated, and I could only imagine what she went through to get this far.

"I know, dear, but your sanctuary isn't too far away. We need to get there now." I didn't want to scare her, but the magical barrier didn't extend this far out. I couldn't protect her and fend off those chasing her.

I wrapped an arm around her as she wrapped an arm around me, and I helped her back up to her feet. She wrapped her other arm around her large belly.

"How far along are you?"

"I'm not sure. Five months, I think. Maybe more."

"Okay. Let's try and pick up the pace."

I didn't want to alarm her, but my keen sense of hearing had picked up a few yips and growls, which sounded like they were yards away. They were closing in on us fast. I whispered a few words, inciting a spell, and threw my free hand back toward the wolves.

One of the wolves yelped, and the woman glanced over her shoulder and nearly stumbled. "Oh, I can't go back," she cried.

"And you're not going to," I said, trying to comfort her. "We're almost there. Twenty more feet."

She seemed to have found a renewed spirit of energy, and we made it across the boundary. Within seconds, the first wolf hit the invisible wall shielding the sanctuary, letting out a loud yelp when it zapped him.

I let go of the woman, spun around, and glared at him. "You won't get her. You can tell your pack master I helped another one." The wolf growled in response, and I couldn't help but sneer. I hoped the wall zapped him well.

The wolf shifted into a man just as two other wolves approached. He glared at me, and I could sense his hate for me radiating from him. "You can't stay behind your magical wall forever, witch."

"You honestly don't know me very well."

At that, he smirked, "We'll be back and in larger numbers."

"And I will be better prepared, so thank you for the warning," I said, giving him a sarcastic grin.

It seemed to have pushed a button as he snarled at me, showing me his white teeth as they lengthened into long, sharp canines. The woman next to me whimpered as she tapped my shoulder. I could sense her fear. It was thick, and I'm sure it gave these wolves a heady rush. The man shifted back into his wolf form, and they all turned away and ran back in the direction they came from.

"I'll be waiting," I shouted, knowing they heard me. It was foolish to poke an angered wolf with such words, but I didn't care. They were sick in the head and needed to be taken out.

My cabin was reasonably nice in size and was as comfortable as I could make it. A few years ago, I was able to install solar panels as I was entirely off the grid. It allowed me to install lights and a small fridge. However, I still cooked my meals on an old wood-burning stove.

I helped the woman settle into bed in one of the three spare rooms. "You know my name."

"Yes, I think a lot of the pack knows you. I overheard them talking about you one day."

"I'm not overly popular with them," I said and let out a small laugh. I honestly didn't care. They weren't fond of either me or my mother.

"I could tell. It wasn't the first time that I heard your name, though. The mother of the daughter I tutored told me that if I ever found myself in trouble, I should find you, and you would give me sanctuary."

"Where's the girl you tutored?"

"I helped her escape. It was the reason why I was locked up. The alpha was furious at Gemma and me and told me I needed to help the pack in other ways for breaking my trust."

"That's how you became pregnant?"

"Yes," she said. Her voice cracked as tears fell down her cheeks.

"Hey," I said softly, sitting on the edge of the bed. I took her hand in mine, "You're safe now. You and your baby."

She squeezed my hand, and I knew that comforted her. "Thank you. She told me you were a witch. I didn't know how powerful you were. I mean, why didn't they attack or follow us?"

"This place is heavily warded against werewolves. They are a very rowdy pack who needs to be stopped, and my place needs to be well guarded if I were to protect anyone who came to me. So, you know my name. What is yours?"

"Sophia," she said softly.

I took a moment to look her over. She was a lovely young woman with caramel-colored skin, maybe in her early twenties. She had brown eyes and long brown hair that looked like she hadn't brushed it in a while. She had scrapes across her arms that

I was sure came from running through the thick brush. Blood began to scab up already, but they needed to be cleaned to keep an infection from sitting in.

"Sophia, I am going to mend these cuts on your arms, and I would like to check on your child to see if they are okay. When was the last time you had eaten?"

"It's been a while. I had been kept in the basement for so long that I had lost track of time. I didn't know if it was day or night until I stepped outside to make my way here."

"I'll be right back. I'm going to collect a few things and see if I can get you something to eat. Just relax. You are safe here."

"Thank you." She laid her head back on the pillow and closed her eyes. I could see her body relax as if she knew she was in the right place. Safe.

I walked out of her room, down the hall, and into the bathroom, where I kept my first aid kit and medical bag in the bathroom closet. One of my mom's requests was that I had gotten an education that benefitted others. I had gotten a nursing degree, but I also studied botany and a few other useful courses in helping others here at my sanctuary.

My mom didn't ask for me to come back here. I chose to come back. What she did here was important to me, too.

I heard some shuffling noises when I made my way to the kitchen. My eyes brightened when I spotted a familiar face.

"Mera," I said cheerfully. "You're back."

"I hope I got everything on the list," she said as she emptied a paper bag. "I had to improvise with a few things." She glanced up at me and smiled. "Do we have a new arrival?"

"Yes, and she's a few months along."

"Blessed be," she said in a cheerful tone. "I'll make her something to eat. I'm sure she'll need it."

Mera was someone who had also escaped the neighboring pack. However, she wasn't pregnant when she arrived, only severely attacked. She was close to death's door, and I was thankful that she pulled through. She was one of a few who decided to stay here and assist me. Mera had no supernatural gifts, but she was a great cook and an excellent nurse's assistant.

I cleaned Sophia's wounds and got out my stethoscope. As I placed it on her stomach to listen in on her fetus, I touched her stomach with my free hand and closed my eyes, concentrating.

I couldn't help but smile when I glanced at Sophia and asked, "Would you like to listen?"

"Yes," she said almost too quickly. She put the stethoscope on, and I returned my hand to her stomach.

"She's healthy," I said, my eyes watching hers. She didn't disappoint me as tears fell down her cheeks as she listened to her baby's heartbeat, probably for the first time.

"I'm having a little girl?"

"Yes, and she is going to be so loved as you will be a great mom."

"I'm scared for her."

"I know, but you got to safety in time, which is all that matters now."

"Her father is a werewolf. I just don't know *who* the father is." Her voice cracked when she continued, "It could be the alpha's. He got mad at me for helping his daughter escape."

"Hey," I said calmly, taking her hand in mine. "You don't have to explain. I understand. He doesn't have ever to know. You can stay here as long as you need to, or my friend Mera and I can help you find somewhere else to go."

Mera stepped into the room carrying a tray at the sound of her name. "Hi. I'm Mera. I've brought you something to eat."

Sophia's eyes darted to Mera. She tried to offer Mera a smile, but her emotions were all over the place. Sophia wiped her cheeks with the back of her hand as the tears continued to flow.

"Why don't we give you some privacy?" Mera exclaimed softly. "Eat and get some rest. We'll be right in here if you need anything."

Sophia couldn't reply other than nod. I found a box of tissues on the dresser and handed them to her before stepping out behind Mera. Closing the door behind me, I followed Mera into the kitchen, feeling absolute hate for that pack and what they did.

Mera turned her attention to me as if she could feel the anger radiating from my pores. "Hey, don't go doing anything rash."

"Why not?" I said in a sharp tone. "How many more will it take for them to come to their senses finally? We know they don't have any."

"Look, I know you're angry right now, but going over there will not help you or that woman."

"They need to pay for what they've done, Mera," I snapped. "You, of all people, should know."

What Mera didn't know, however, was that I vowed to get back at the pack somehow. I grew tired of how horrible they treated women. I knew the pack and their pack master only through association. My father was the pack master until the current one challenged and killed him. My mother escaped because she was in trouble.

My mother was a powerful witch who fell in love with a werewolf and then she met my father. She said he wasn't that great of a man, but he tried to be for her, and that seemed to make him weak in the eyes of his pack. He was challenged and lost his life. She said she knew the alpha who took his place and was terrified of him. The moment she found out he was coming after her, she left.

Even though I was half-werewolf, I didn't know anything about pack laws or rules. My mother never talked about it or my father. She created this haven for her and me and vowed to accept any woman who needed sanctuary, even if it meant sneaking them away from the pack in the middle of the night. She had helped many women through the years. Some of them stayed, some had passed away during childbirth, and some had left to find their ways out in the world far away from here.

Once I came back here to help my mom keep her vow, my mother left for a time only to return to show me that I had a sister, Lissa, who was half-dragon. They stayed for a time and left, never to return.

I thought about my mother and sister, wondering where they were. My sister would have turned nineteen or twenty not too long ago and probably came into her shifter abilities already, if not "earlier.

Mera walked over to me and wrapped her arms around me as if that would help calm me down. "What do you want me to do?" she asked, knowing that no matter what she said, I was going to war with this pack.

"I may need you to help me watch Sophia."

She stepped back and met my gaze. "I can do that. When are you leaving?"

"I'm not sure yet." I wasn't sure. I hadn't thought this through. "I may wait until it gets dark and check things out. See if I cannot find any weaknesses."

"You'll need to stock up on your energy," she said encouragingly.

I was fortunate to have Mera here with me. She kept me on my toes and reminded me to eat when I skipped a meal because I was too occupied with something.

4

John

Paul and I had arrived in upstate New York without any issues. However, after securing a car, I began to feel nauseated. Once we passed through the gates of the pack, I was feeling nervous about taking over as temporary alpha in my brother, Aiden's place. I could sense that we were being watched the closer we got to the estate.

As if he could sense my uneasiness, Paul said, "Hey, John, you'll do fine."

"Thank you, man. That's supposed to be my line," I said, letting out a small laugh.

"It's only natural for you omegas to feel nervous or scared. I am here for you," he said, reassuringly.

"I can only hope my brother knows what he's doing."

"Are you questioning Aiden?" he joked.

"My brother, yes. My pack master, also yes. I wouldn't be his pain in the ass if I didn't," I laughed.

Paul knew I would never question my brother in public. It wouldn't be the first time I had to consort with Paul on his thoughts when it included anything to do with the pack. However, Paul was the only person I had ever discussed anything concerning our pack master since Paul was the third in command.

"I would never question our alpha, but I am concerned about his choice for his replacement."

"Me?"

"No. Your cousin Vince. He hasn't been around in almost a year and doesn't stick around for more than a week or two."

I nodded my head. "Let's only hope that Vince has changed."

As we approached, I saw several pack members standing outside near the front door. The moment I stepped out of the car, I was knocked back with a mix of negative emotions. Anger was thicker than all the rest, but I understood why the pack felt this way. Aiden killed their pack master and told them an omega was standing in for him to be their alpha.

I didn't want to say anything out loud for fear of one or all the pack members hearing me, but I silently hoped that Vince would show up sooner than expected. I was confident that I wouldn't live that long if he didn't. I know Paul was strong enough to take on at least two, maybe three, but not the whole pack.

As we approached the front door, I could hear a few low growls and some grumbling. This was going to be fun.

"Meeting in twenty minutes," I said to them. "Tell everyone to be here."

When I walked inside, a young male, who appeared to be in his early twenties, approached me. Paul instantly stepped in front of me, blocking the young male's path as he not only radiated hate and discontent, but his face and body posture shouted it.

"You're not welcome here," he spat.

"Meeting in twenty minutes," I replied as calmly as I could.

An older male stepped out of a room, walked over to the young male, wrapped an arm around him, and smiled at me. "You'll have to ignore Brett. He's harmless."

"He needs to learn to show it," Paul replied sternly. "And not approach as if he's challenging another wolf, or he'll soon learn his place."

"Brett, why don't you take a walk outside," the older male said and turned his attention to me. "I'm George. I can show you around if you would like." He extended his hand, and I shook it. "Your office is down the hall. However, I should warn you, someone has already stepped up to claim their role as pack master."

"Seems like we have a problem already, boss," Paul told me without taking his eyes off George.

"Take me to him," I replied coolly. I knew that something like this was going to happen.

The moment we walked into the office, my stomach churned. I wasn't prepared to be challenged. I wasn't one to accept one if I were. The male behind the desk sneered, and Paul responded with a growl that rumbled the room. It was more of his claim as the pack's alpha, and I felt like tucking my tail and running, but I stood my ground with my head held high.

"I've already staked my claim as alpha, and the pack already voted on it," said the male, furrowing his eyebrows as if we interrupted him.

"I hate to be the bearer of bad news," I said and released a sigh of irritation. "But the Council doesn't want anyone from your pack taking any officer roles. I'm in charge for the time being until your appointed pack master arrives."

He jumped out of his seat, and Paul let out another deep growl, causing the offending male to step back. His eyes showed a glint of yellow around the irises, his fingernails and canines extended. Paul must've triggered him because this self-appointed alpha was close to shifting. I didn't want to be the one who he challenged as he was much bigger than me. However, he wasn't nearly as big as Paul who was nearly seven foot tall.

"The Council can't do that," the posing alpha snapped.

"The Council can and will. That's why they are in charge," I replied, keeping calm.

"No omega is going to take over this pack," he growled. "I am and will and have. So, the two of you are going to leave."

"You are going to back down," Paul said. A low rumble reverberated deep in his chest. It was a commanding move that made it obvious as to why he should be the pack's alpha and not me. When the offending male didn't move, Paul said sharply, "Obey your alpha or find yourself in contempt."

"How are you going to run this pack if you have to have someone else barking your orders for you," the male laughed, turning his attention to me. "I'm not sticking around, and neither will the rest of us."

I shrugged nonchalantly, "Then you can leave. But I should warn you, don't think about starting your own pack. The Council released a statement that you would be held in contempt should you do so. You can claim rogue status but you must leave the region when you do or you'll have a bounty on your head."

He scoffed, "Leave this region and go where?"

I shrugged again, and said, "Anywhere but this region. I should warn you though, my pack is on the West Coast, so you don't want to go there. My pack master was the one who took your alpha and his second down without any issues."

When the male opened his mouth to speak, someone wearing only ripped jeans burst through the door, panting, followed by two other males dressed similarly. "We lost her, boss."

"Lost who?" I asked him.

Ripped Jeans turned to me and narrowed his eyebrows as he ran his gaze up and down. "Who the fuck are you."

The male behind the desk said sarcastically, "Supposedly our new alpha."

The three intruders fell into a roaring laughter as if they had heard the funniest joke.

"You didn't answer my question," I roared over them. I didn't attempt to exert any authority. I was too tired mentally and physically, but they were being loud and rude.

The man behind the desk smirked and said, "It's none of your damn business."

Paul was over the desk the second the self-appointed pack master had gotten the last word out of his mouth. Paul had the male pinned against the wall, his arm pressing against the male's neck, choking him. The three intruding males growled loudly and began tearing away the rest of their clothes to prepare to shift.

Paul spun the male around so fast I just stood there with wide eyes, unsure which guy to take down first. Paul had his arm around the male, pulling him up off his feet, and the male was clawing at Paul's arm as he was visibly struggling to breathe.

"Back down," Paul roared through his lengthened canines.

He was so commanding even my wolf was cowering, begging me to leave the room. This was how I pictured things going once we arrived.

"Back down," I shouted when I finally found my voice. I glared at the three males, wondering if they would listen. They froze but continued to bare their canines as a sign of showing me that they were still a threat.

Paul loosened his grip around the male in his arms and said quietly, "Leave." He glanced at the three males and said, "All of you."

"You're banished from this pack," I added, "and are hereby given rogue status. Pack your stuff and leave this region."

I waited until they were gone, and I turned my attention to George who was crouched in a corner. I didn't blame him for not wanting to get caught up in this mess.

"I need you to stay for a few minutes."

"Sure thing," George replied as he stood up.

"Would you mind explaining to me what that was all about?" I asked George as I sat down on the edge of the desk. I was thankful I had something to brace myself on as my body was still shaking with adrenaline.

"A woman they were holding prisoner had escaped recently."

My brows furrowed in confusion. "Why were they holding her prisoner?"

"She broke the former pack master's trust and helped his daughter run away. They were tracking her, but if they returned emptyhanded, she made it to the witch."

"The witch?" Paul asked, leaning against the doorframe. I imagined it was his way of standing guard in case someone else came charging into the office.

George let out a breathy laugh, "Oh, yeah. You have a lot to learn here."

"That I do. So, tell me about this witch and where I would find her."

"She won't be too happy if you bother her. She's quite powerful, and her place is well-warded against our kind."

"I insist. I want you to take me to her. I need to make amends for the crimes this pack has done. Send out an olive branch."

"I can do that, but I won't take you the whole way. As I've said, she's quite powerful and doesn't like us very much."

"I'm guessing this pack has angered her to the point she's had to take things into her own hands."

"It's gone back to when our last alpha took over. He killed his pack master. That pack master's mate was a witch. She ran away and did all she could to take in women that escaped from here."

"Oh, wow! I can see why she's angry. Her mate was killed."

"They had a child together and that child is the one who lives there now. She's more powerful than her mom ever was."

"You do realize that we can't treat women that way anymore. We have laws to follow."

"You won't have to worry about most of the pack standing against you when you proclaim the new laws to be obeyed. When the last pack master had taken over, most of us were too scared to challenge his rules. Some pack members were as ruthless as he was and had the same way of thinking as he did. Our pack did grow in numbers, but at a cost."

"How long will it take to assemble everyone for a meeting?"

"Not that long. Most of the pack lives nearby. A few others had stepped out years ago as they disagreed with how things were going here. You can call them, but you may have to make personal trips to visit them."

"I'm enlisting your help to call everyone local. I'll need everyone else's phone numbers. I'll give them a call and let them know what's going on."

George stepped out of the office, and I could feel the stress weighing on me. We hadn't been here thirty minutes, and it was already a clusterfuck.

"I hope you didn't mind me stepping in like that," Paul asked.

"Not at all. I was glad that you did."

I was sure that Paul should've been the one that Aiden sent, and I had half a mind to tell my brother that. I pulled out my phone and hit his number on the speed dial, but it went straight to voicemail. I didn't bother leaving a message. Aiden would have seen that I called and would get back to me.

"You know, I am glad you are here," I told Paul. "No way I could have handled those guys, let alone one."

"Hopefully, it'll be the last we hear of them," Paul said as he walked over to the window and stared outside.

"I hope you're right," I replied, and my phone rang.

"Are you going to let Aiden know how well things are going here," Paul laughed.

"What do you think?" I replied with a smirk and answered the phone. "I sincerely hope Vince is going to pull through," I told my brother.

"Well, hello, brother," he snapped. "Guess you're still alive long enough to get snarky with your alpha."

"Oh, no," I laughed. "You're the one who put me in this position. The pack put someone in charge when we got here, and that isn't all the trouble I've experienced. I'm thankful Paul was here, or I wouldn't be."

"I gave Vince a call and he is on his way."

"He can't get here fast enough," I sighed.

"That's why Paul is there with you, little brother."

"I'll call you back in a while. I have to go break the news to the rest of the pack and find a missing woman."

I rubbed my head as I felt a headache forming caused by stress. How did Aiden do this as an alpha? It was different when I stepped in for him to take over our pack when he lost his first wife. Maybe it was because we were all linked, bonding us together in a way. That made it easier for me to be in charge. It wasn't enough experience for me to take over this pack, even if it was temporary.

"Missing woman?" he asked, surprised.

"Yeah," I said sarcastically. "But you already knew they held them captive here. I've yet to investigate how bad it was. A woman had run away shortly before we got here, so I need to see if I can find her and check on her wellbeing."

"I didn't know anyone was being held prisoner when I was there. Keep me informed," he replied before ending the call.

The pack meeting didn't last twenty minutes. Only twenty-two of the supposedly fifty-five-member pack showed up. George informed me that a few pack members stepped out, saying that they were leaving the pack. It wasn't looking good, and if that wasn't bad enough, I asked George to show me where the runaway woman was being held. I wasn't prepared for what I saw.

I contemplated taking this position. An omega had no business taking a role as alpha, especially a pack master to a pack of callous wolves still stuck in the past. What I was looking at was more than barbaric. The stench of sickness and bodily filth about knocked me over once we entered the basement.

I couldn't believe what Gemma told my brother Aiden and me about her father and his pack. Now I was here to see it for myself, and I was stunned.

I know Aiden was trying to protect his young bride without getting involved with this pack. This was why I don't foresee him leaving the West Coast any time soon. Another reason why is that Gemma wouldn't go back due to all the trauma she had endured at a place that was supposedly her home.

"They locked them up down here," George stated, snapping me back to attention.

"And, what? Forget that they're down here?" I asked.

"Partially," George replied.

"I think I've seen enough," Paul added, unwilling to take another step inside the room.

At 6 foot 10, Paul was a bear of a man with muscles, and his wolf was certainly not something you wanted to make an enemy with. He was in charge of our security team. And, right now, I could feel that he was as sick to his stomach as I was. I couldn't agree more with Paul either. It was nauseating how they treated anyone down here.

"I want this place cleaned up. This place should only be used for rabid wolves, not holding women hostage so that they can be bred. That's not how things will be done from here on out."

We had used large cages to house the wolves who were lost mentally — where they were too far gone and unable to return to their human form or what we called rabid. Moon sickness was part of it or severe trauma.

The only time I could remember when we last used ours was when Aiden and I were little, and our Uncle Ben was suffering from severe PTSD. Our father kept Ben locked in a cage. He gave him the best care he could considering Uncle Ben's condition. He had reverted to his wolf form and was feral.

I don't know what happened to Uncle Ben. We weren't supposed to be down there, as our father said it wasn't a place for children. When we were caught sneaking down there, our father punished us severely. It was the last time we had seen Uncle Ben.

"They kept the women down here and had their way with them until they were pregnant," George said, snapping me back to the present.

"Did they at least get medical treatment?" Paul asked.

"We have a doctor on the payroll."

I walked past the first cage and asked, "Where was the runaway staying? I'd like to get her scent and see if I can pick up her trail."

"Over there," George pointed. "The far cage."

It had to be the furthest one, forcing me to walk past all the others. Thankfully, they were all empty. I stepped inside the cage and picked up a pillow. It was small, dirty, and raggedy but would carry her scent the most.

"Do you know which way she went?" I asked George.

"West towards the witch's house."

"Paul, I want you to take care of things here. George, I would appreciate it if you would help him while I'm gone. I'll try to get back as soon as I can. If this witch is as powerful as you say she is, I want to try and make peace with her. She could be a useful ally"

"Good luck," George chuckled.

I stepped outside, headed towards the house's eastern side, and began removing my clothes. I dropped the pillow and shifted into my wolf form. It was easier to scent and track this way. Once I had gotten a good whiff of the pillow, I headed east. Her scent was faint, but it was a start.

It had been a while since I had been in my wolf form. It was freeing, getting to run, and feeling the ground beneath my paws. Even though it was temporary, I enjoyed the freedom away from the estate. I knew Paul could handle anything for me while I was away.

I paused to sniff the air and along the ground. Her scent was getting stronger, telling me that I was getting closer, but it was a maze getting through the wooded area as it was covered with thickets and brush.

By the time I made it out of the woods, I could see a cabin, but what stopped me was an invisible barrier. The second I hit it, I was zapped, causing pain to rip through my whole body and eliciting a yelp from me. The barrier also had some sort of an electrical pulse that had knocked me out momentarily.

5

Kara

Sophia was in and out of consciousness. Her wounds weren't that bad, but she needed to see a doctor soon to determine how far along she was. Depending on which trimester she was in determined her chances of survivability. Only a small percentage of human women survived going into the third trimester.

As I waited for nightfall, I stepped outside to gather a few things from our garden when I saw a gray wolf with white socks running toward the cabin. I stood up and watched him run into the invisible boundary, becoming trapped. He changed into a man as if his shifting would help him to escape, but it was useless. I couldn't help but sneer. This wasn't one of the wolves I recognized from earlier. I had never seen his coat markings before, and I wondered if they just sent someone else to try my patience.

"Well, now," I said as I approached him.

He glanced up and watched me with pleading eyes. I raised my hand toward him, whispered a few words, and watched as he bent over, yelling out in pain as the boundary zapped him with electricity. I could also hear his wolf whimper. This spell was equally harmful to both animal and man so they would remember the boundary was here and know not to trifle with me.

I moved my hand down, releasing the spell. "Why are you here? You can't have her," I spat out, wanting him to feel my rage.

He tilted his head as if curious about what I said. "I only wanted to check on her wellbeing," he said softly.

I raised my hand and chanted the spell again, watching him writhe in pain. "Nice try, wolf."

"I'm the new alpha," he groaned as another electric spark zapped through him briefly. "The temporary one until my cousin shows up." I began to repeat the words, but he shouted, "Please, believe me when I say I have come in peace."

I lowered my hand and said sternly, "I don't believe you."

"I know, but I simply came to talk peace," he said, and as I raised my hand to zap him again, he shouted, "My brother killed the alpha, and the Council has sent us to make changes. Please, I don't mean you any harm."

His words came out rushed, as if he needed me to hear him before I zapped him again. I knew he was in pain; I could smell it, as well as sense it. I also knew he wasn't an alpha. There was no way. An alpha wolf wouldn't give in so easily.

"Killed the alpha, huh?" I wondered why the alpha didn't come for the woman herself or his second in command. "And Foster, his second?"

"Yes, my brother killed both."

"Your brother must be a powerful alpha."

"He is. Please, I came because I want to make peace with you. I don't wish you or the woman any harm. I want to help."

He flinched as I leaned closer and sniffed him. He smelled different. "You want to help?" I asked in a sharp tone. "Were you the one who forced himself on her? Or did you watch?" I already knew the answer but wanted to hear him say it.

"I didn't know about her till a half hour ago. I simply came out here to check on her. No ill intentions or harm will befall her. You have my word."

I sniffed the air again, but deeply this time, and I could sense he was being genuine. He also didn't smell like the pack I was dealing with. His scent was nowhere on Sophia.

"I feel I can trust you, but only for a moment. You try to pull anything, wolf, and you'll soon regret it."

He chuckled and massaged his head after I released the boundary's hold on him. "I already got the feeling I would, quite painfully." He extended a hand toward me and said, "I'm John Trenton."

"I'm Kara," I replied, shaking his hand.

The moment my hand touched his, my wolf stirred. She was quite taken by John and could sense he was decent. He was certainly not lying when he said he was new to the pack. I had gotten a visual that he was from somewhere else. I was intrigued by him, as was my wolf. We wanted to know more about him.

"Where are you from, temporary alpha?" My intuition picked up West Coast, but I needed him to be more specific.

"Oregon state."

"And your brother isn't here to take over? I thought the one who killed the pack master took his place?"

"Tricky thing about that. He's already the pack master of the Oregon Territory, so the Council forced him to name a replacement."

"You called yourself temporary. Is someone else planning on taking over then? You said your cousin?"

"Yes, my cousin Vince. He's making his way here. I know things between you and the pack aren't that great, but you have my word that things are changing. They can't harm you anymore."

I scoffed, "Oh, but they will try."

"They would have to answer to the Council if they tried."

"Please excuse me if I have a hard time believing you." I knew the wolves that came here earlier. They would undoubtedly hold to their word and would be back. It was a matter of when.

"I know it's hard, but you'll have to trust me at least to try and fix things. I heard you were a powerful witch and have experienced that myself," he laughed. "My wish is for you and me, the pack, to become friends. Allies."

"I will have to think about that."

"Okay. That's a start," he chuckled. "May I please see the woman?"

I paused for a moment before I answered, "You may, but if you try anything—"

"I know," he interrupted with a soft laugh, "you'll hurt me."

"You're going to need clothes before you see her," I pointed out.

My eyes ran over his naked form, and I couldn't help but smile inwardly. I didn't want him to see I enjoyed taking a peek.

"Oh, right," he said, finally realizing that he was in the nude. He rubbed the palms of his hands against his legs and seemed as if he was a bit embarrassed, which was awkward for a werewolf. "Uh, I left my clothes back at the house."

"I have some sweatpants that might fit you. Why did your brother put you in charge? You don't seem like alpha material."

"That's because I'm not," he said as he ran a hand through his dark locks. I held my hands up, and he flinched. "I'm an omega," he exclaimed.

I couldn't help but let out a loud laugh. "Wow! I haven't seen one of you in a while. I thought that's what you were. You're submissive."

"Not completely," he winked, and I got the impression he was trying to flirt with me. It was cute, but I was still unsure who he was.

"I'll take you to see her," I said, shaking my head in amusement.

I honestly couldn't remember the last time I had seen an omega wolf. I think I was little, and it was actually a woman. She had come to this sanctuary for help. She was one of the few who survived giving birth to another werewolf simply because she was one. Not many women shifted into wolf form. I was one of the few who could and so was she. Too many of us had blurred DNA that prevented a lot of things.

The only way to become a werewolf was to be sired by one through breeding. When males began mating with human females, genetics began to thin out, and pack numbers began to dwindle. It was one of the reasons why the New York pack's alpha was trying to grow his numbers.

If the two-natured kind — shifters and weres — didn't save their species, they would go extinct. In my opinion, that wouldn't be such a bad idea.

6

John

My stomach churned as I watched her move closer to me as we walked toward the cabin. I could see it up ahead and was glad it wasn't too far of a walk. There was something about her that I couldn't place. She frightened me and interested me at the same time, and that was a first for me. I stuck my nose in the air to pull in her scent, and my wolf stirred, and my heart jumped. *Mate.*

There is no way, I told my wolf. I took a deep breath and released it, hoping it would clear my thoughts, but it didn't. It only brought in another whiff of her scent. It was earthy, with a hint of vanilla. I couldn't stand her being angry at me. I certainly needed to get her on my side.

I cleared my throat and said to Kara, "I can feel the magic surrounding this place."

"It's heavily warded," she said with a smug smile. "It's to protect all that I allowed within the boundary and keep those who wish to do harm outside of the boundary."

I gave her a reassuring nod, "I like that." I did like that she could protect herself, as well as others, against harm. I could've come up with something better than talking about magic, but apparently, my brain couldn't function. I wanted to impress her. Get her to like me for the sake of becoming allies, but I feel like I wanted it for other reasons.

"Would you like some tea?" she asked me as soon as we were inside.

"I'd love some," I replied.

By the time I had slipped on the clothes she had given me to put on, the tea was ready, and she had everything set out on the kitchen table.

"How long have you been here?" I asked as I sipped my tea. It tasted a little different than what I usually drank, and as I took another sip, I felt the warmth spreading through me like a blanket, comforting me.

"For a long time. How long have you been here?"

"I just got here a few hours ago." I took another sip, feeling more relaxed. "I wanted to check in on the woman."

"She's resting now. What is your business with her?"

"I wanted to make sure she was okay," I replied and cleared my throat. My answer felt forced from me, somehow. "I simply want to help," I added, but those were my words.

I stared at Kara momentarily as a smile broke out on her face. She couldn't have poisoned me, would she? My eyes darted to my cup, and I struggled to form the next question. "What did you put in my drink?"

"Just some herbs to help you speak the truth," she smirked.

"But I've been nothing but truthful from the start."

"I know," she shrugged. "I had to make sure. You can't be too careful."

I shook my head as if it would help clear my thoughts and break this spell she had me under, but I was feeling fuzzy. My wolf was certainly not happy and was fighting it just as much as I was.

"What did you think of me when you first saw me?" she asked.

"That you were beautiful," I replied and then clapped a hand over my mouth to avoid saying any more. I drew in a deep breath and then struggled as I asked, "When will this wear off?"

"Hard to say. Each person is different. It also depends on how strong you and your wolf are." She stared at me for a moment as if waiting to see how I would respond. "Do you know the woman who escaped your pack?"

"No, and not my pack," I replied with a slight growl.

"I thought you said you were the alpha."

I drew in another deep breath and let it out before I answered. "Temporary alpha."

"Who is the new alpha, then?"

My body ached as I fought to tell her I wasn't the bad guy, but again, I answered her question truthfully, "It's my brother, but he sent me to take his place until his replacement shows up."

"When will that be?"

"I don't know." It was the truth. I winced as the supposed truth serum continued to run its course. I needed the control of my own awareness to return. She continued asking questions as quickly as I answered them, as if her magical herbs would wear off within minutes. I hoped they would.

"How do you not know?" she asked sharply as if my answer offended her.

"My cousin Vince shows up on his own time. He was given a few weeks to take the position. Until then, I'm stuck with it."

"What do you think about how your pack treats women, Temporary Alpha?"

My brows furrowed at her question. I hated how the former alpha did things here. "Horrible. That's why I was sent here. The Council is trying to make changes within the pack." My body shuddered as I fought to gain control of my senses. My chest rumbled as my wolf growled, showing his displeasure.

"Somebody seems displeased," she said with a breathy laugh.

"Do you have a piece of paper and a pen?" I asked through clenched teeth and watched her reach into a kitchen drawer behind her. She pulled out a notepad and pen and handed it to me. "This is my number. Should you need anything, please call me. I seriously want to help."

I left it lying on the table as I stood up and stared at the door momentarily. I wanted to go but wasn't sure if I could. I didn't want to get zapped again.

I turned my attention to her and asked, "May I leave?"

"Yes, but only if you wear this." She walked to one of the cabinets and pulled something out. "I'm not sorry for giving you the herbs. If you had been in my shoes, you would understand why I had to do it. I have a hard time trusting anyone from that pack. This place needs to be protected at all costs. The women that come to me need to be protected."

She held her hand out, and I stared at the object in it. "It isn't easy for me to give out my secrets, but I feel like deep down I can trust you. Wear this, and you can get through the ward without trouble."

The moment my hand touched hers, I felt an electrical spark go through me. It must've happened to Kara as well, as she flinched and glanced up at me with a shocked expression that matched mine. My wolf also stirred, as both of us were curious about what transpired.

I sniffed the air just once, a quiet gesture, but I needed to know. My heart rate picked up as soon as I picked up her scent. It was funny how my wolf caught it before me, but maybe it was because I was used to helping others and not looking for anything that benefitted me.

Kara continued staring at me as if she was expecting me to make the first move or speak first, but I was too stunned to. I listened in and could hear her heart rate go up as well as her breathing. She knew what had happened. I couldn't make that step unless she were on the same page as me. It would hurt more than anything if she denied this.

My hand slowly moved to touch hers again, and she didn't pull away. That spark I felt earlier rushed through me again, stirring every part of my being. It was thrilling to experience this for myself finally. It wasn't nearly the same feeling as when I first discovered Aiden's mate. But now ... I wanted to howl excitedly.

I cleared my throat, "I, um, I," I stuttered. My words seemed stuck in my throat, or maybe the magical herbs were still coursing through my veins, causing my mind to feel muddled. "May I see you again?"

She smirked, her eyes darting down as if she was too embarrassed to answer. "We'll see each other again."

"Drinks will be on me," I smirked, and she let out a soft laugh.

I stepped back and put my thumbs into my pants to prepare to shift back into my wolf and paused. As odd as it seemed for me as a werewolf, I couldn't let her see how hard she had made me. "I'll take these off outside," I said with a small laugh and turned, making my way toward the door.

The moment I stepped outside, I slipped the necklace on, and slipped out of my pants. I folded them neatly and placed them by her front door, and then shifted into my wolf form, feeling ecstatic. My wolf shook himself as if that would help get rid of the magical spell faster, then jumped elatedly before taking off in a full run back to the pack's estate.

7

Kara

Mera stepped in through the back door, and I could already hear the smirk on her lips before she spoke. "He was an interesting guy." By interesting, she meant good-looking. I shook my head, which caused her to chuckle. "What? It isn't every day we have handsome guys visiting us."

"Not every day," I replied in a playful tone. I was busy laying out my herbs to prepare them into salves and oils. It was a careful practice that I've done many times, but still, I didn't care to be interrupted.

"Well, nice guys anyway," she added, coming to stand next to me. She paused briefly before speaking again. "So, how nice was he?"

"He was okay," I answered, knowing she wanted me to go into detail as to why he was here.

She was just like any other woman who needed her next fix of gossip and drama. We had plenty of drama already with every woman that came through here. John's visit was certainly something different.

"He seemed nice enough to be able to make it in the cabin and then make it out alive. What did he want?"

"He wants peace," I said, even though I knew that would lead to more questions.

"Clearly, he isn't from our favorite pack."

Calling the pack, we've had nothing but trouble with our favorite, was a joke, but it was one of the names we used to call it.

Turning away from my task, I faced Mera and sighed, giving her my undivided attention. This was something that I was happy to report. "He's not from that pack. He's from another pack and standing in as the temporary alpha."

"Well, that is good news," she said boastfully. "Hopefully, we can get peace after all. Is that the only reason for his visit?"

"Not really. He wanted to check on Sophia and offer his assistance in anything we needed help with. After ingesting a little truth serum, he was not lying about his intentions."

"I think we should take him up on his offer to help. We could use it, especially since it's his pack, new or not, that has caused us so many problems. Do you think his wolves are done harassing us?"

"Guess we'll find out."

"What does that mean for our sanctuary then?"

"I'm not sure." That was an interesting question I didn't think about until Mera mentioned it.

"We're both trained as midwives. It wouldn't hurt for us to continue helping in that capacity."

"I wouldn't be moving in with the pack if that's what you suggest," Mera replied, and she had every right to say that.

"Not what I meant. There are plenty of opportunities outside of the supernatural realm."

"That's true."

I honestly hadn't thought of that either. Mera and I were completely capable of working in the human world. She had done it before she had gotten involved with the pack and for a short time after, yet she chose to come back to help me. Would this new alpha truly bring change? Was John's cousin on the same page as he was? And did that mean my work was here was done? I didn't know. We had been dealing with that horrible pack for so many decades that we didn't foresee anything like this coming.

"I guess I would have to talk to this new alpha again," I said.

"Oh, you know you want to. At least have him come here so I could get a good look at him," Mera joked, eliciting a boisterous laugh from me.

I shook my head. "You just need something nice to look at, right?"

"Maybe," Mera jested, giving me a wink. "At least you're finally admitting that he's nice-looking."

"I didn't say he wasn't," I said with a small laugh.

"You didn't. But you didn't admit he was until now. At least take him for a few rounds in the sheets."

"You are a mess, Mera," I said, shaking my head.

"And I'm sure he has your hormones all over the place," she joked.

"Oh, from the sound of it, that's what he's done to you," I replied with a smirk. I didn't want to tell her what my wolf thinks of the newcomer. Mera, for sure, would be picking on me nonstop. I needed my time for peace and quiet. I also needed time to think about some things.

I also needed time to reassess the fact that my wolf thinks John was our mate. I couldn't just accept that without getting to know him better. His new pack was to blame for that. I don't date. I just don't. Not to say that I wouldn't be interested. I've never had time for it. He did look very lovely without his clothes and seemed well enough endowed for me to sneak a few glimpses.

I don't know what it was about male werewolves and being well-equipped, but I had never seen one that came with small packaging. Now, I couldn't say anything about the human males because I knew quite a few that didn't have anything worth bragging about.

I shook my head to try and clear my thoughts. Both Mera and my wolf had me thinking about sex and the lack thereof. It had seriously been a while, and yes, my hormones were acting up after John's visit.

"I need to gather some more herbs," I said, feeling flustered.

Mera couldn't help but let out a cackle. "Somebody sure has you hot and bothered."

"No, I just need some more herbs."

"Girl, you have enough herbs all over the counter there. You just need to cool off. Maybe you can catch a whiff of him if his scent is still lingering."

I grabbed my basket off the top of the fridge and stepped outside as quickly as possible to avoid listening to her blather about her nonsense. Mera knew I was half-wolf and one of the few females who could shift. I wanted to leave before she started asking what my wolf thought. Thankfully, Mera hadn't bothered asking about it. Hopefully, she wouldn't. I was done talking about the subject altogether. Being outside would not only give me some fresh air, but it would give me the quiet I needed to think.

8

John

Whatever Kara put in the tea seemed to have worn off by the time I returned to the estate, as my mind felt clearer. Gladly so, as I made it back to the office, the so-called self-appointed alpha was again sitting in the chair Paul and I had evicted him from.

Glancing around the room, I noticed his thugs weren't around, and it was just him and me in the office. I thought about reaching into my pocket for my cell phone and calling Paul to come up here, but I had tasked him to find help in cleaning up the dungeon. I drew in a deep breath and slowly released it. I could handle this on my own.

"I thought I told you to leave," I said sharply.

"I felt inclined to return since you went after something I want," he replied smugly.

He was leaning back in the chair with his hands behind his head, his tailored shirt taught against his chest, showing off his muscles. My eyes met his. He was watching me curious with a smirk. I surmised he was calculating how quickly he could make it over the desk and have me on the ground. He wouldn't do it, though.

"I told you that the Council doesn't want anyone from this pack to be alpha. That's why I'm here." I stood there in the doorway with my arms crossed, irritated that I had to repeat myself.

"Oh, I'll be alpha. Maybe not here, but I'll take some of my pack with me."

"I already informed you that you can't do that. This isn't your pack anymore."

"Watch me," he growled, dropping his hands on the desk with a loud thud. I seemed to be poking the beast, and rightly so. After taking a tour of the basement, I was angry enough to shift into my wolf form and take a few swipes at this brute.

"You'll be eradicated. It will be a death sentence for you and those who follow you."

"Doubt it," he snorted. "But that's not what I was talking about."

"Do tell then," I said, leaning against the doorframe.

"That woman is carrying my pup."

"Oh, so you're admitting to forcing yourself on a human woman then?"

He let out a breathy laugh through his nose. "I'm not the only one. The pack master had her the first week. Then, after he left, I took her and made her mine."

"So, she's your mate?"

"Not even close," he snorted.

"Well, she isn't yours then. She's a human and they have laws. The Council had updated our laws, too, so you should know you've broken quite a few of them."

He let out a snarling growl, his eyes turning a golden hue. He was on the verge of shifting, yet I stood there, keeping calm. Any sudden change in my mood or a sudden movement could have him shifting and possibly ripping my head off.

"The pup she's carrying is mine," he said in a deeper voice, showing his lengthening canines, "and I'll have it even if I have to take matters into my own hands."

"That isn't happening," I replied casually. "That woman is under my protection and the Council's. You have been banished from this pack. I've already notified Council of your status."

At least now I knew who abused the woman in Kara's care. I was trying to keep my cool and not tell him what I thought of him. I was against forcing a woman into doing something she didn't want to do, especially forcing a human woman to breed against their will.

He stood up and slowly approached me, scowling as he did and showing me his mouthful of sharp teeth. I stood there, unwavering, my arms crossed, my face relaxed, my heartbeat even. I wasn't about to back down because he attempted to intimidate me.

He stopped within a foot of me. His huge frame towering a few inches above me. Could he take me on and win? Sure. He was more muscular than I was and an alpha wolf, but he wasn't going to because the Council would order his death if he did. That would get in the way of him getting what he wanted. I seemed to be a roadblock that was in his way. I was here on official business, and he was interfering or attempting to.

He huffed through his nose when I didn't bother to look up or back away. "I'll have that woman, and you or the Council won't stop me."

"Should I tell the Council to go ahead and order your execution then?" I asked, taking a chance to direct my gaze to his.

He snarled and huffed again. His wolf was gesturing and on the verge of taking over, so I knew they were both on the same page. Instead of answering me, he shoved his way past me, pushed me out of the way with his body, and left.

I released a deep sigh through my mouth and walked over to the desk. I needed the Council to be updated. If there was ever a Cover-Your-Ass moment, this was it.

"Shit!" I shouted. I didn't even know his name. I needed to ask George about that, and he was busy.

Secondly, how do I inform the Council that a human woman is carrying a werewolf? I promised to protect Kara and those in her sanctuary. By telling the Council, I would have to indulge her whereabouts. Kidnapping and breeding human women went against our laws. The Council knew what this pack was doing. That's why I was here — to put a stop to it. But now I had an angered wolf who admitted to forcing himself on a human woman and getting her pregnant. She needed to be protected at all costs, and so did Kara.

Kara was not only a witch, but she was also a wolf. I could smell it. She wasn't part of any pack but her own. She was an alpha in her own right but was off the radar, meaning the Council didn't know about her. If I reported the woman to the Council, I would also have to report Kara.

"Fuck," I swore under my breath. I wasn't sure what to do, and that wasn't like me. I always did what was right and followed the rules. "All right," I said out loud as I picked up my cell phone, "I'll do what is right."

9

Kara

A smile tugged at the corners of my mouth. Mera may be a pain sometimes, but at least she was honest. True, it didn't hurt to have a nice male figure to look at for once, especially one that didn't result in us having to fight. That was a huge bonus.

I shook my head as I replayed the scenario between John and me, and my wolf stirred. Was she lonely? Was I? I didn't know what I wanted other than helping these women out. But did that mean I wouldn't have to worry anymore now that John was here to help? Should I look for a job now that I won't have one here?

I needed to talk to John further and try to come up with a plan. I was sure that wherever our kind resided, they would need a midwife and a healer. It wasn't normal for us to go to a human doctor or to attempt to go to a hospital. We couldn't let them know about us.

I was too caught up in my thoughts to have heard someone sneaking up behind me. By the time I heard him, he was already leaping towards me, pinning me to the ground with my hands in front of me. He quickly placed a hand over my mouth, or I would have cast a spell on him. I squirmed to throw him off, but I could tell he was enjoying himself as he dug his hardness into my backside.

"That's right, bitch," he growled in my ear, and I knew who it was — Warwick.

I recognized his voice as one of the troublesome members I had dealt with before. Was he the one who sent those wolves earlier? One of them did promise they would be back. I was kicking myself for being too distracted.

"Keep moving," he cooed. I mumbled something, and he laughed, "No way am I stupid enough to remove my hand from your mouth. You are going to listen to me talk, though."

I tried to push myself up off the ground, but he was too heavy, and the more I moved, the more I could feel him pressing into my lower back.

"I have to admit," he said hoarsely in my ear, causing me to flinch from his hot breath, tickling my skin. "I am enjoying this. I finally have you where I want you. Underneath me."

He shimmied himself lower, placing his erection at the crevice of my behind, and began rocking his hips. I moaned in disgust and jerked my body in an effort to get him to move off me, but it was useless. It seemed to make matters worse for me and more enjoyable for him. I was wearing leggings and could tell he wasn't wearing anything. He must've shifted into his wolf form on his way here.

"I could take you so easily, but you're lucky I'm not interested in you right now or I would. You already know what I want, don't you?" he asked, and I nodded. "You're going to take me to her. Try anything stupid, and your girlfriend will get it."

My heart skipped a beat. Did one of his thugs have Mera? I thought she was in the cabin. Did she leave and go somewhere? I didn't know if he was telling the truth or not. I felt pinpricks hitting my cheek and flinched. His nails must've elongated, pricking my skin.

"Put your arms behind your back," he huffed.

He got up on his knees and pulled me up with him. I began to bring my arms back but jerked my body forward to free myself from him. I needed his hand off my mouth to cast a spell, but it needed to be quick. His hand slipped for a moment, but I wasn't fast enough.

"Nice try, bitch," he laughed and dug his claws into my arm with his free hand. I hissed in the palm of his hand. "Give me your other arm, or I'll make it hurt worse," he barked.

Not once did I ever think this day would come when one of my enemies would have me at his mercy like this. I put too much trust in the shield that was put up. How could I have let my guard down? I tried to think of how it was even possible that a werewolf broke through the barrier, but it was hard to think when one of them had his claws pressed to my neck and could simply kill me with one slight move of his hand.

Warwick escorted me into the cabin, where another man was waiting with Sophia. They were seated at the table. Sophia was crying and shaking. She was visibly terrified. The man with her was not a wolf. He was … human. Of course. A human could walk through the barrier. It was this person that helped the wolf inside, but how?

"Kara!" Sophia cried when she saw me being held hostage.

I wanted to say something, comfort her, and let her know that despite how things looked, I wouldn't let any harm come to her. I struggled to speak, but only muffled sounds and groans came out as Warwick's large palm was still clasped around my mouth.

The human hit Sophia's head on the table, knocking her out. "We're going for a little ride," he said with a mischievous grin.

He walked up to me, and I watched him remove a collar-like device from a bag slung over his shoulder. When he approached me with it, I flinched, but Warwick grabbed my head and held me still while the human put the collar around my neck, locking it in place with a click.

"You can let her go now," the human told Warwick.

Warwick released me giving me an evil chuckle that sent my skin crawling. My heart raced, and I immediately tried to cast a spell. I half-expected that it wouldn't work. The moment the human put the collar on me, I felt my powers dampened. Now, I was terrified. I'd never heard of such a thing that could prevent a witch from using her powers. It was terrifying to imagine. I felt utterly human, not being able to feel my powers. It was very disconcerting as I couldn't even feel my wolf.

The human laughed. "The collar prevents you from using any spell," he said. "You also won't be able to shift." I looked up at him and glowered, and he chuckled. "Yes, I know you are half-wolf. The collar will keep both parts of you in check."

"Please, Sophia needs me," I begged, as I could only appeal to them now.

If she were as far along as I thought she was, she would need as much help as she could get to keep her alive. Most humans didn't make it to their third trimester carrying a wolf's pup, but if she did, and she needed to be monitored to ensure that she would make it the rest of her pregnancy.

The man put a cloth in my mouth to gag me, and then I felt strong hands around my neck. It was Warwick. He squeezed, and it was all I could do to struggle against him.

As consciousness escaped me, I heard the human say, "Well, you're coming with me, as my payment."

10

John

I was in my office discussing the future of the pack with George when a woman suddenly barged in.

"How did you get in here?" George asked, visibly alarmed that a woman, who was clearly a human, would boldly walk into wolf territory uninvited. I was equally surprised, considering the pack's attitude toward them.

The woman was sweating profusely, and her breathing was hurried and heavy. She had been running, but from whom, I wondered. Or what? She ignored George's questions and strode toward me. She placed her hands on my desk, trying to catch her breath to speak.

"You said you would protect us," she managed in a breathy, raspy voice, her eyebrows narrowed as she glared at me. "You are doing a shitty job at that."

"Who are you?" George asked more firmly, demanding the woman's attention.

She looked at George. "I'm Mera," she said. She turned back to me and said, "Kara's closest friend."

When I heard Kara's name, I sprung up to my feet, sending the office chair crashing against the wall behind me. "Did something happen? Where is she?"

"I saw them from far away," Mera said. "From the woods. It was one of the wolves we've dealt with before. Big burly guy. Three wolves came to the sanctuary earlier this morning and threatened us."

"It was probably Warwick," George muttered. "He's the one you dealt with up here who was appointed the new alpha."

So that's what his name was. My wolf was struggling to be set free. He and I both were ready to end this wolf's life.

"He is nothing but trouble," George added. "As you've already found out."

"They put a collar around her neck. Another man was helping Warwick, but he wasn't part of this pack that I know of.

At least, we haven't dealt with him before," Mera said. "They took Kara and Sophia away in a van."

"Hold on. Who is Sophia?" I asked.

"She's one of the women Kara saved who was impregnated by one of your wolves," Mera replied.

"Warwick is claiming the pup as his own," George said under his breath and sighed. "It's why he sent some wolves after her."

"He told me as much," I replied, and George tilted his head in confusion. "He came back up here. He must've gone to Kara's after he and I had some more words. We have to find them," I said. "Do you know where he would go?"

"They could be anywhere. Warwick knows this city more than the rest of us. He can easily disappear anywhere," George said. "He spent a great deal on the phone with someone I'm sure was outside the pack. He was hoping to organize something, but I wasn't sure what. He's met with a human up here many times, it could be him."

"Mera, what did this man look like?"

"He was tall, blonde, athletic," she replied.

"That sounds like him," George added.

I turned to Mera, "Anything else can you tell us that would help?"

"There was a … another vehicle. A black SUV. It followed the van."

"Did you catch the plates?"

Mera shook her head. "I was too far away, so there was no way I could see it clearly."

"Okay. Do we have anyone on the police force we can trust?" I asked, turning to George.

"No. Most of them are corrupt, loyal to Burk the previous alpha, the one your alpha killed." George cleared his throat, and I noticed his hesitation before he said the next thing. "I do have a brother, though, Philip. He is a wolf, but he works for the FBI in New York City."

"With a possible human antagonist involved, it's no longer just werewolf matter. We will need the law involved. Contact your brother. We need to do whatever it takes to find them."

"On it," George said.

"Introduce Mera to Philip so she can help him profile the human and come up with a sketch of him. While we will do our best to find Warwick, Philip can help us find the human. That way, we will work on two fronts and get to Kara and Sophia sooner." When I finished talking, the room was quiet for a minute. Mera and George were staring at me, and I couldn't tell what the expression on their faces was. It did look like respect.

George nodded. It was a kind of nod you'd give a leader you believed in. It felt good.

He glanced at Mera briefly and told her before he left the room. "I need to go make that phone call."

I walked around my desk to meet Mera, and I embraced her. "You were brave. You did well." She held on to me tightly. Her heart was beating fast. Not only could I hear it loudly, but I could also feel it against my chest. I closed my eyes, drew in a deep breath, and focused on using some of my omega magic to soothe her.

"She believes you are different. A good wolf," she said. "Don't let her down."

Her words were like cold water touching my skin, gripping. I was getting emotional. We'd only met once, but Kara had become too important to me, like my second half. I guessed that was what mating was like.

"I will get her back. I promise," I said, and I meant it. I would do anything in my power to get her back.

11

Kara

I opened my eyes and let out a soft gasp. The first memory that appeared was Warwick gripping my neck from behind. I immediately tried to get up. Something forcefully pulled me back into my seat, and I hissed in pain. I found that I couldn't move. I'd been chained to the bed. It was wrapped around my arms, pinning me against the railing of the bedframe. I peered over to my shoulder and saw Sophia lying on the bed. She was still asleep. Good. She didn't need to be awake and stressing right now.

I glanced around the room. It was small with only a dresser, bed, and bedside table. We must have been in a small house. The door stood wide open, and I only surmised that for safety purposes on our captor's part. A sound coming from the doorway had me turning my attention to it when Warwick walked into the room with a stupid grin. I wanted to slap it right off his face.

"I did not introduce myself earlier," he said. "Forgive my manners. I'm Warwick, but I think we've met a few times." He held up a plate of food as he if was the waiter bringing our dinner. "This for you. You must be hungry. I can imagine it isn't every day a powerful witch like you gets kidnapped by a wolf." He smirked, and I wished I could cast the spell I was thinking in my mind right now and have his ears melting. But this damn collar around my neck, whatever it was, wouldn't let me.

"You must be wondering why I took you with me. I need you to ensure she delivers my pup safely," he pointed at Sophia. The audacity to claim to be a father to Sophia's child sickened me to my bone.

"I have not had a chance to have a doctor check her out yet. Have you?" I asked.

He scoffed. "That isn't my job."

"No? But it is. You got her pregnant. You want to be the father of her child; you need to step up."

He growled, and his eyes changed color, "Don't tell me what to do, woman."

I shook my head and let out a soft laugh. "I guess it hurts your masculinity too much to help a woman out, even though you put her in the position she's in."

"You're lucky I need your help," he snapped.

"Or, what? You'll hurt me? You need me," I smirked. I knew I was testing his patience. Good. He'll get his in the end. I would ensure it.

He sneered and threw the plate of food down in front of me. The way the plate slapped the floor caused the food to splatter. "It was your idea that I take you with me anyway," he said, taking in a deep breath as if he was trying to calm himself.

"Where is the human?" I asked.

"He is of no significance to me anymore. He got me what I wanted. Rest assured, he is the least of your problems."

Warwick walked closer to me and crouched in front of me. He was so close; my chest was in his face, and I saw the way his eyes darted from my face to my boobs each time my chest rose when I drew in a breath. He grabbed my thighs firmly. I tried to maintain a calm look, not to let him see that he affected me negatively. That way, I intimidated him subtly.

He smirked and released me, then he reached for a chain that I didn't see located under the bed. One end was attached to the bedframe while the other had a cuff on it, which he clamped onto my left ankle.

He released the chain that was wrapped around my chest and arms, allowing me to breathe freely without feeling

83

constrained. Warwick's eyes went straight to my breasts, and he grinned mischievously before directing his gaze to meet mine.

"If you hope to survive, you will do as I tell you, Kara. For your own sake, that baby better be safely delivered." He looked down between my legs and looked up at my face, and he smiled and then got up. "Or you'll replace her," he added before leaving the room.

After he was gone, I took a deep breath and let it out slowly. I faced the ceiling to prevent the tears that were starting to cloud my eyes from falling. *Fuck*, I muttered. I really could use my mother's help right now. I shut my eyes tightly, allowing old memories to wash over me. I remembered how mom trained me in the art of casting spells. She taught me everything I knew. She also taught me to be strong. And that was why I had the willpower to stand up against these wolves. I was able to save many women because of that. But now, who would save me, I wondered.

I glanced over at Sophia. I was sure that she would be due any day now. Why would Warwick be interested in her so much? I needed to be strong for her. I couldn't let her see me weak.

Sophia began to stir.

"Sophia," I muttered. "Hey". I had a feeling she believed all that happened was a dream. And now she would wake up to the realization that it was, in fact, all real. I would need to calm her before she got overwhelmed and her baby became distressed.

She looked at me. "Kara," she said softly, and she sat up. Then she noticed that I was chained to the bedframe. "Kara?" She squinted her eyes, confused.

"Hey, Sophia, I'm fine, okay? Just don't overthink."

"Where are we?" she looked around. The realization was starting to set on her. She was beginning to remember. I could already see tears forming in her eyes. "Oh my God. We were attacked."

I could hear her heart beating fast.

"Sophia, you need to calm down, or you'll hurt your baby," I said sternly.

"My baby," she cried, looking down at her big stomach and caressing it.

"You need to be strong for your baby, Sophia. You don't worry about any of this. I will get us out of here, okay? I promise."

"Kara," she muttered under her breath.

"Do you trust me?" I asked. She nodded swiftly. I smiled at her. I gave her my hand, and we locked fingers tightly.

I felt like my heart would burst. I was overwhelmed, but I was keeping my emotions contained. It was hard. In truth, I was clueless about what to do. I felt so helpless without my abilities. But I had faith that something good was going to happen. All I'd ever done was save people. I had faith that a savior would come now that I needed to be saved.

My mind went to John.

He will save us.

"Why did they put the collar around your neck?" Sophia asked, snuffing.

"It dampens my powers," I answered.

"How?"

"I don't know. It must have been built with a special kind of magic. I've never heard of such a device, though I'm sure others like me can create such an object."

"Have you tried removing it?" Sophia asked.

I looked at her. It had not occurred to me to try. I believed I couldn't remove it if they put it on me. The collar must have had preventative measures so I couldn't remove it.

"I'm not sure that would be a good idea," I said.

"You're not going to try? If there's any hope of getting out of here, it would be with your witch powers," Sophia said.

I sighed. I still thought it was a bad idea for me to remove the collar, but I had to try, at least to please Sophia. I put both hands on the sides of the collar, tried to summon my wolf strength, and pulled. As soon as I pulled, a pulse flowed out through the collar and seeped into my skin from my neck down. I let out a sharp cry, panting as it continued to pulse through my body.

It wasn't an electrical shock per se. It felt like someone lit a match inside me, and my innards caught fire at once — like a deep, melting sensation. It scared me enough that I was confident it would lead to my death if I continued to try and pull it off.

Weakness consumed me, and I was blinking in and out of consciousness.

And in the middle of that, I fell into a trance as a vision popped up in my mind. I saw a redhead with fair skin. She looked young and beautiful. And she was looking at me. One moment, she was smiling, bright-eyed, and the next, she looked angry, and there was blood all over her face, and then, before my eyes, she began to shift.

She was a dragon, and she was beautiful. I had never seen one in their true form.

Who was she, and why did I have a vision of her? Was she my sister, Lissa? Would I finally get to see her? Why was I having a vision of her now?

I had so many questions. Every time I had a vision, it was something that was going to happen. Only, I wasn't sure when.

12

John

I hurtled through the woods toward Kara's cabin in wolf form. I hoped the necklace Kara gave me would enable me to move through the protective barrier without any issues. I wanted to get a sense of whatever happened and see if I could pick up a scent trail.

I wasn't sure when I went past the barrier. I didn't feel anything if I did. I knew I must have been close as her cabin was in view. I began to sniff around, trying to pick up Kara's scent. It wasn't hard. Her scent was everywhere. I supposed I should try to pick up Warwick's, as well to see if that was really him. I had his scent already.

Wolves had a strong scent, and due to my abilities, I could block out scents and narrow in on one. I could also determine emotions through someone's scent. Even though we all don't have the same scent, it should be easy to distinguish a wolf's scent from that of a human and a witch.

I trotted around a bit before catching the scent I sought. I tried to stay with it and followed it to an area close to the cabin. Warwick's scent and that of Kara's were strongly mixed up. He must have been all over her. That thought alone had gotten both me and my wolf angry. But that wasn't what got me enraged.

Everyone's scent changes when they are usually aroused, and I could tell Warwick certainly was. I could ascertain through Kara's scent that she was furious, and I'm sure it was because this wolf had not only gotten the best of her, but he was assaulting her, and she was helpless in defending herself. I let out a growl and snarled, baring my fangs. I was going to make Warwick pay for what he did.

He must have covered her mouth to prevent her from casting any spell. I didn't know her well, but I was sure she would not have let him take her or anyone from this place without a fight.

My fur stood on end, as I imagined his hands all over her as she fought him with all her energy. I had never felt like this before. I have dated before, but I have never ached as much as I was at this moment, and I supposed that was how it was with mates. My body and my heart hurt. Kara had been kidnapped, and she and that other woman were in danger, and I didn't know where to turn to look for them.

Kara had become very important to me in the short time I had been with her, and whatever happened to her affected me tenfold. I'd seen what being kept from one's mate could do to a wolf. I was a little lucky that my fate and Kara's had not particularly been sealed yet. Still, I was getting increasingly uneasy. Indignation was swirling within me, threatening to blow me up from inside. My wolf was agitated, making my body shake uncontrollably. The images of tearing Warwick to shreds flickered in my mind as the only means to pacify my wolf.

My investigation wasn't over yet. I still needed to go through the cabin and out front, where Mera said she had seen the vehicles. As I made my way through the cabin, I shifted into my human form and fell on my knees, trying to catch my breath. I was struggling. There were too many scents and so many mixed emotions in here that my head was spinning. I shut my eyes tightly, focusing on Kara until she was all I could see. Our last meeting replayed in my head. I remembered her smile. I remembered how our skin touched for that brief moment. My heart was beating as fast as it did then, but for a different reason.

I opened my eyes and took several deep breaths, steadying myself. I couldn't afford to allow myself to become overwhelmed at this point. I needed my head in the game. I needed to be thinking straight. That was the only way I could ever hope to find Kara.

I walked around for a bit, looking around for clues and thinking. I wondered what Aiden would do in this situation. I contemplated calling him, but I changed my mind. He wouldn't expect me to run to him at every problem if he made me the alpha here. As much as I didn't like any of this—being an alpha to this particular pack, being in New York, away from home, and what I was familiar with—I didn't think I was anything close to alpha material, but I wanted to do my best to be up to the task and lead.

I had the brains. I knew I was smart. I could handle this situation myself. Besides, this was Kara, and whether we bonded or not, she was my mate. Of what use was I if I couldn't save her myself?

The cabin seemed empty. I wondered where Kara kept all the women she saved. They must be safely hidden somewhere around here, or was there another building I couldn't see? Or perhaps she had relocated them out of town?

How was Warwick able to get to Sophia? I had a feeling there was someone on the inside, some of the women Kara saved, who was still loyal to the wolves. I needed to talk to Mera to see if we could figure out who that might be. Hell, it could be Mera herself. *Fuck.*

I shifted back into my wolf form and began trotting into the woods. I couldn't focus on picking up anything else here. I needed to see Mera and properly interrogate her. I thought I'd made a mistake not doing that earlier; instead, I let her go with George to meet his brother.

I put Paul in charge of the pack while I was away. Officially, as alpha, I could do that. Aiden be damned, I was calling the shots. Paul had already stepped up and was doing the work. He was doing a great job, too, keeping the wolves in line. They feared him, and that was good. Wolves would follow whoever they feared and respected. However, loyalty was birthed from genuine love and respect.

I'd seen how loyal Paul was to Aiden. It wasn't because he feared Aiden. It was because he had great love and respect for him. I had a feeling a great battle was inevitable. We would need as many wolves as we could rally and control. So, Paul's influence was priceless. I truly hoped that they knew how bad it would mean for them if they chose Warwick. He sealed his fate the moment he kidnapped Kara and Sophia.

As I strode along, I caught a familiar scent. I stopped immediately in my tracks when I saw him. He was in his wolf form, running toward me, but stopped several yards away. When he shifted, I recognized him as the one who bursted into the office when Paul and I arrived. I banished him along with Warwick.

I shifted to my human form, too. I needed to cool my nerves before I spoke so as not to come off bitter.

I drew in a deep breath and released it before I asked in a calm tone, "Do you want to die?"

I wasn't sure why he was still lingering around. It was unnerving that he was still here. It was also against the rules. I could have him killed for this alone, but his scent wasn't malicious.

"I see you've made friends with the witch," he said.

His tone was humbled, as opposed to being the arrogant wolf that seemed to urge me to challenge him when we first met. From his statement and his unwillingness to step toward me, I surmised that he was standing right behind Kara's magical barrier, unable to walk through.

Out of curiosity, I walked a few steps closer, stuck my nose in the air, and sniffed, catching his scent. He wasn't involved in Kara's kidnapping, that I knew of. I didn't smell his scent anywhere on her property. Yet, he was sent here this morning by Warwick to harass her.

"What do you want?" I asked, not willing to move any closer.

I couldn't risk stepping out of the barrier if that was what was stopping him from coming closer to me. I was still unsure where it ended exactly and only took a chance by guessing I was close to it. I wasn't able to smell the magic lingering in the air as I did before right as I got caught in Kara's trap. Was it still there or did the necklace block it?

There was no one around to save me if this wolf here decided to fight me after all. And there was no way I could beat him. He was much bigger than me, and I was not a great fighter like my brother Aiden. We were also deep in the woods, a perfect place for him to kill me and bury me and pretend like he didn't know anything.

He placed his hands on his hips and shifted his weight to one foot, his body posture relaxing, which told me he was not here to fight. He sighed after staring at me intently for what felt like an eternity.

"My name is Seth and I'm not here to hurt you," he said. "I came to tell you that you must stop, Warwick."

I was surprised to hear him say this. I knew he was being sincere, without ill intentions, because it took him great effort to say those words.

"He is involved in something even I cannot stand," Seth added.

"What is it?"

He hesitated before speaking.

Seth's eyes flickered with a mix of anger and disgust as he revealed the sinister truth about Warwick.

"Warwick has this unholy alliance with a druid, and they have a nefarious plan to create a hybrid army by breeding with every species and creature imaginable."

The sheer audacity and malevolence of it all sent shivers down my spine.

Listening intently, I could feel Seth's growing determination to personally end Warwick's abominable scheme. His clenched fists and resolute gaze betrayed his unwavering resolve. It was clear that he saw himself as the last line of defense against this unholy union of witchcraft and bestial perversion.

I couldn't help but share Seth's revulsion. The very thought of Warwick's twisted ambition made my stomach churn. The world was already full of dangers and uncertainties, and now we faced the prospect of an army of unnatural creatures unleashed upon us all. It was a nightmare come to life. Such an army could potentially bring the Council down, which was probably what he intended to do.

"John," he said, his voice steady and resolute, "I promise I will stand by your side until Warwick is brought down. We will put an end to this madness together. I hate that we got off on the wrong foot. The only reason why I came out here earlier today was to try and talk to the witch, but Warwick sent others to help me, but it was to grab Sophia and bring her back. Warwick needed to stop."

"I appreciate your candor. I believe he kidnapped Kara — the witch and Sophia. Did you know she was carrying his pup?"

He shook his head as if he was in disbelief. "I do, and I will help you find him and bring these women home."

He shifted into his wolf form and bounded back toward the pack's base. I also shifted into my wolf form and followed, but to take precautions, I stayed several feet behind.

When I arrived back at the main house, a heavy sense of unease still lingered within me. Who else was involved in kidnapping Kara? I wasn't sure where Seth had gone, but I needed answers, and Mera, Kara's closest friend, was the next person I had to confront.

Finding Mera, I approached her cautiously. "Mera, I need to talk to you," I said, my tone firm. "I need to know if you had any involvement in Kara's abduction?"

Mera's eyes widened with a mix of surprise and fear, her innocence evident in her gaze. She stuttered, denying any knowledge or involvement, but I needed to be sure. The gravity of the situation demanded that I employ unconventional methods to uncover the truth.

Drawing upon my omega instincts, I allowed my primal energy to surge forward. My body trembled, and in an instant, I shifted into my wolf form. The room was filled with an aura of wild power as my gaze locked onto Mera's widened eyes.

With a low, rumbling growl emanating from deep within my chest, I circled her, my movements calculated and deliberate. Every step I took was designed to unnerve her, push her past her limits, and extract the truth.

Mera trembled, her breath coming in shallow gasps as she backed away, confronted by the immense presence of the wolf before her. The fear in her eyes mirrored the situation's intensity as her resolve wavered under the weight of my primal display.

Her body froze as I sniffed her. I hated scaring her, but this was the only way to find what I wanted. My senses keenly attuned to any signs of deception; it became clear that Mera knew nothing about Kara's kidnapping. Her fear was genuine, her innocence undeniable. The truth finally revealed itself in the depths of her eyes, but it also answered something else.

I shifted back into my human form, the tension in the room dissipating. Mera's trembling subsided, and she met my gaze with a mixture of relief and lingering fear. It was then that I realized the toll my actions had taken on her, and a wave of remorse washed over me.

She flinched when I approached her, but I assured her with my posture that it was with a gentleness that contrasted sharply with the previous intensity of my wolf form.

"I apologize for having to show you my true form. It isn't a method I would use around humans, but I needed to ensure you were telling me the truth. You are innocent."

"I tried to tell you I wasn't involved."

"I apologize for any fear that I have caused you. I picked up a few scents at your cabin. I didn't find them on you."

"I don't know who they are other than that one wolf. I'm not involved in this in any way."

"I believe you." I paused for a moment before I spoke again. I wasn't sure if I should tell Mera, but surely, she would understand if I did. "I know you and Kara are close, but she means something to me, too."

Mera, still shaken, managed a weak smile as if she understood what I meant. We both knew the magnitude of our situation and that unwavering loyalty and trust were paramount in our pursuit of justice.

Together, we were united in our determination to bring her back safely. The encounter with Mera had provided clarity, eliminating one potential suspect from our list. It was a small victory amidst the chaos, but it bolstered my resolve to find the truth and ensure Kara's safe return.

Leaving Mera to recover from the ordeal, I set off again, focusing on the next steps in our investigation. The truth was out there, waiting to be discovered, and I would not rest until Kara was found and those responsible were brought to justice. I needed to call Aiden and give him an update. He would have to call the Council if he hadn't already. I wasn't sure what the Council had planned for Warwick, if anything.

As the weight of the situation pressed upon my shoulders, I retreated to my room, seeking solitude and a moment of respite before calling my brother. Just as I settled into the quiet, George entered with a sense of urgency in his eyes.

"John," George spoke, his voice filled with a mix of concern, "I have news from the my brother. While you were out, Mera provided them with a description of the human who aided Warwick in Kara's abduction. They've initiated an active search for him. My brother has started his investigation on Warwick, too. Apparently, he is a person of interest. "

My heart skipped a beat at the news. "What do you know about Seth?"

"It's hard to say where his allegiance lies. He's a great wolf. Dominate. He wants to be a good pack member and help his pack master, who he may be. I think Warwick was using him. He was one of the wolves who ran into the office when Warwick was here."

"I ran into him again," I said.

"I thought you banished him."

"I did. Seems as if he was determined to pass along a message. Warwick is working with a druid. That's probably who the human is. I picked up an interesting scent at Kara's that reeked of magic, but it was definitely set apart from Kara's kind of magic."

I wasn't sure what it meant. I could tell the person had the gift, but he didn't smell like a witch. I had never met a druid before to be able to distinguish if that was what I smelled or not.

"I'm sorry, I can't help you there. My sniffer stopped working years ago."

"Thank you, George, for the update. I need some time to decompress. I had gotten myself a bit overstimulated."

"Sure thing, boss. I'll give you some quiet time to yourself," he said, and escorted Mera out of the room.

As the others filed out, I closed the door behind them, allowing the weight of the moment to settle within the confines of my mind.

Now, alone, I paced back and forth, my thoughts racing as I mulled over the information. The FBI was informed, but I knew all too well the limitations of their investigation when dealing with those from my world involving themselves in the human world.

The FBI operated within the boundaries of human law, while our pursuit of justice was unrestricted by such constraints. It wasn't rare that our two worlds collided. In fact, it has become an enormous problem that I was sure would grow into something too big for our kind to deal with.

However, it was the first time that I had someone in the FBI who was from my world helping us. I wanted to think that it was a good thing.

I was becoming overly anxious. Maybe the quiet wasn't such a good idea. My wolf and my mind were both telling me that I needed to be doing more. I wasn't sure what just yet.

13

Kara

Sophia's bloodcurdling screams pierced through the fog of my unconsciousness, snapping me back to reality. As I gradually regained consciousness, my senses struggled to comprehend the chaos around me. My vision was hazy, and the distant echoes of Sophia's frantic shouts reverberated in my ears. I strained to make sense of my surroundings, and my mind clouded with confusion.

Amidst the disorienting blur, I discerned the sound of hurried footsteps drawing closer. A figure materialized before me, reaching out to lift me from the ground. Though their face eluded my grasp, I instinctively knew it wasn't Warwick.

Suddenly, an injection pierced through my skin, its contents flooding my veins with an intense potency. The substance coursed through me, rapidly neutralizing the debilitating seizure that had overtaken me during my futile attempt to free myself from the collar's grip. A profound sense of relief washed over me as the medicine took effect, easing my pain and granting me respite from the grip of the collar's torment.

Despite the newfound relief, my body remained weak and unresponsive, rendering me unable to move. Either overwhelmed by exhaustion or from the drug I was given, I succumbed to unconsciousness once more, drifting into an abyss of darkness.

When consciousness finally reclaimed me, it was as if I was emerging from the depths of a haunting nightmare. I jolted awake, gasping for air, my heart pounding hard against my chest as I struggled to orient myself in the unfamiliar surroundings. The room gradually came into focus, and there stood Sophia, her tear-streaked face a poignant blend of relief and worry.

"Kara," Sophia called out, her voice filled with joy and her eyes filled with concern. I turned my gaze towards her, my eyes meeting hers. A flicker of a smile graced her lips, a testament to her immense relief at my awakening. "I thought you were going to die," she whispered, her voice trembling.

Seeing Sophia's face, witnessing the genuine concern etched upon it, brought a measure of solace to my weary soul. With a sigh of gratitude, I allowed myself to sink back into the confines of the chair, surrendering to its support. The weight of the collar's power still gnawed at the corners of my mind, constantly reminding me of the dire consequences that awaited any further attempts to defy its hold. I felt like I was going to die.

"Don't blame yourself, Sophia," I uttered weakly, my voice barely more than a strained whisper. The toll of the ordeal I had endured was evident in the fragility of my words. "All of this is on me, and I will find a way to free us from this nightmare. I only ask that you remain strong for your baby." I wasn't going to try breaking the collar off me again.

Even as I spoke those words, my resolve wavered, my shaken state betraying the inner tremors coursing through my being. The memory of the collar's unforgiving power lingered, casting a shadow of doubt upon my ability to overcome this perilous situation.

I closed my eyes and pictured John, trying to call out to him subconsciously. I truly needed him to find us. *Where are you, John?*

My eyes flew open when I heard the bedroom door creak open. The human who put the collar on me accompanied Warwick into the room. His presence commanded attention and having them both inside this room only made it feel smaller. I was too tired to fight either of them.

"You're awake. Good," the human greeted me.

I don't know why I didn't pick up on it before, but his voice carried a subtle Irish accent that added a touch of intrigue to his words. Walking towards Sophia, he extended a hand and gently placed it on her forehead to assess her condition.

"I hope you survive the birth of your child. You are … not in good shape," he uttered with genuine concern laced in his voice. "But you've made it this far for a human, so there's some strength in you."

My protective instincts flared, and I couldn't help but interject, my voice brimming with urgency. "Get away from her," I urged, reflecting my deep-rooted worry.

To my surprise, the human responded with a disarming smile, his expression betraying a sense of understanding.

"You should be more concerned about yourself. You were at death's door. I pulled you back," he revealed, his words carrying a weight that made my heart skip a beat. "You will need your strength to help Sophia deliver her baby. Your failure might mean her death, and that wouldn't look good for you."

As I studied him more closely, it became evident that there was something extraordinary about the man before me. His mere presence exuded an enigmatic aura that eluded comprehension. The flicker of recognition danced at the edges of my mind, hinting at a familiarity I couldn't quite place. The thought crossed my mind: could he be a witch, too? Such supernatural origins would explain the mystique that seemed to envelop him.

My eyes glanced over at Warwick standing in a corner, watching us, and I turned my attention back to the human. "Why are you working with this wolf? And not just any wolf.

That man is pure evil, and you know it," I voiced my concerns, my voice laced with a mixture of indignation and curiosity.

A calm expression settled on the man's face, his eyes holding a glint of knowledge that sent shivers down my spine. "And what do you think that makes me?" he responded, his voice maintaining an unnerving calmness.

His words echoed in my mind, causing a seed of doubt to take root. What if Warwick was not the true mastermind of this operation? What if this enigmatic man standing before me held the true power? I realized that there was far more at stake than the simple act of delivering Warwick's pup.

A chuckle escaped the man's lips, breaking the tension building in the room. "I'm messing with you. Hey, I'm a nice guy. Honest," he reassured, his words offering a momentary reprieve from the weight of uncertainty. "It's just … there's something I desperately need. And Warwick can give it to me. In exchange, I deliver his pup. It's kind of a business deal, see?"

My indignation flared up, fueled by a sense of righteous anger. What did he want from Warwick in return? "You will turn against your kind to help a heartless wolf?" I challenged, my voice brimming with a defiant conviction.

The man scratched his chin thoughtfully, his gaze piercing into my very soul. "My kind? Interesting," he mused, his expression betraying a hint of amusement. "Do you *really* not know what I am? Or are you just assuming?" His penetrating stare seemed to unravel the depths of my thoughts, awaiting an answer to his cryptic questions. "Rest assured," he continued, his voice dripping with a palpable air of superiority, "I am not human."

"I could sense that much," I replied.

A surge of adrenaline coursed through my veins, causing my heart to race. The man's aura shifted, becoming more intense and intimidating, emanating a power surpassing any ordinary wolf. Whatever he was, he possessed an otherworldly strength that both fascinated and unnerved me. The burning question lingered: what could he possibly need from Warwick that warranted such a desperate alliance?

Just as he was about to leave the room, he paused and turned back, his eyes meeting mine again. "Forgive my manners. I am Ciaran. I truly want us to get along," he said, his words carrying an air of enigmatic purpose. "I also want you to know that I am powerful enough to take down the shield protecting your humble sanctuary."

With that, he and Warwick left the room, leaving us to grapple with the mysteries he had brought into our lives. That boggled my mind. Who was he to have that much power? Anger boiled up inside me as the realization of my sanctuary being invaded like that. How would I be able to return to that place now? It was no longer safe for anyone seeking shelter.

A heavy sigh escaped me, and my gaze shifted towards Sophia. Her stare bore into me with a vacant expression, leaving me wondering if she could sense the fear and anger that lingered within me. I had to push these thoughts away. At least for now.

"Hey," I uttered softly, attempting to break the heavy silence that enveloped us.

"Hey," she responded, her voice quivering, a delicate dance of unshed tears evident in her eyes. Despite her apparent distress, Sophia seemed determined to conceal her vulnerability and stand strong. I was proud of her for that.

"You don't have to hold back your tears," I reassured her, my words a gentle encouragement. "It's part of what makes you human."

"Crying won't solve our problems," Sophia retorted with stern determination. "I know that. I won't let Warwick take my baby. So, we must do whatever it takes to escape this hellhole soon enough. I don't want to go into labor here."

Her anger resonated with mine as I surveyed the chain binding me to the bed, clenching my teeth in frustration. Indeed, Sophia was right; escape was imperative. My first instinct was to understand the collar's intricacies, decipher its mysterious workings, and finally free myself from its oppressive grip.

The magic within the collar, designed to inhibit a witch's powers and suppress wolf abilities, intrigued me. It defied my understanding of magical constraints, challenging the boundaries I thought existed. Recalling the forbidden magics my mother had taught me, I delved into my memories, searching for a similar concept that could be repurposed to create a spell capable of temporarily neutralizing a witch's power.

The excitement of potential discovery pulsed through me as I considered the possibilities. My heart raced with anticipation and hope as I mulled over possible solutions. Then, with widened eyes, a realization dawned on me—a breakthrough.

"I've figured it out," I exclaimed, triumph coursing through me. The spell woven into the collar was within my grasp, and with determination, I knew we could unlock the key to our liberation.

As I tried to arrange my thoughts, I heard movement beside me. Sophia was moving uncomfortably in bed.

"Sophia?" I called.

"I think he's coming," Sophia cried, her hands cradling her lower belly.

"What? Now?" I knew she was talking about the baby. This couldn't be happening. The baby was not supposed to arrive for another week or so. Having her deliver her baby now would make things a lot more complicated, and escaping with a baby might be impossible.

Sophia cried out. *Fuck! Fuck! Fuck!*

"Somebody?" I yelled. "Anybody there? Please help! Ciaran!" I shouted at the top of my voice. I needed to be set free to help Sophia deliver. I couldn't help her with one of my hands tied down.

"Oh my, God, Kara. What am I going to do?" Sophia asked.

The tears were flowing without control. She was terrified. I was scared, too. Delivering her baby here, with Warwick ready to claim his pup, Sophia would never have access to her baby again. That kind of stress wasn't good for Sophia or her baby.

Not if I could do something about that.

"Just focus on your baby right now, Sophia. You can worry about other things later. Let's deliver your baby first. Hey, you need to be strong for her. Just think about her and nobody else."

Ciaran came into the room, his eyebrows knitted in concern.

"Hey, you have to release me. The baby is coming now," I said to him. He hesitated, glancing from me to Sophia and back to me. I rolled my eyes and said snarkily, "Take your time."

He raised a hand toward me, touched the collar, and said something in a whisper, a word I didn't understand. The chain used to tie my ankle fell right off. He *was* a witch! But what language was he speaking? There was no time to ponder that fact. I needed to attend to Sophia.

The dimly lit room embraced us, and my heart raced as I fumbled for my next move. It wouldn't be my first time delivering a baby. But this time, I was in so much distress. I had barely recovered fully from the seizure I went through, and now it would seem I was about to deliver Sophia's baby into the hands of evil.

Sophia lay before me, her face contorted with both pain and hope. With a deep breath, I steeled myself for what lay ahead, knowing that Sophia's life and the life of her unborn child depended on my resourcefulness.

I assessed the situation. Though the room lacked the tools I was accustomed to, I knew improvisation was my only option. I gathered a few supplies: a clean bedsheet and towels. Ciaran came into the room with a bowl of warm water. I hadn't noticed he had left.

"I know this isn't where you wanted to give birth," I said to Sophia as I helped her get more comfortable in bed. "But your baby is ready, and I am here to help you deliver her."

With each contraction she endured, I closely monitored her progress, using my hands to assess the position of the baby. It was clear that this birth might be a little difficult. If I had my magic and portions, I could make it easier for her. I felt terrible that Sophia had to go through this.

I gently guided her through each contraction, encouraging her to breathe deeply and find solace amidst the pain. The room was filled only with the sounds of our breaths and Sophia's soft cries. Ciaran stood at a distance, watching with intrigue in his eyes. He looked particularly eager to see the end of all this ordeal.

I used my hands to guide the baby's descent, employing gentle but firm pressure to navigate through the narrow passage. The room seemed to fade away as I focused solely on the task at hand, my instincts guiding me through the intricacies of childbirth.

As the hours stretched on, my determination remained unwavering. I relied on the power of touch and the strength of my own hands, acting as a conduit between Sophia and her precious baby.

Finally, with one final push, the room erupted in a chorus of cries—a symphony of relief and joy. Sophia's baby took its first breath, announcing its arrival into the world. I placed the newborn on Sophia's chest. Their bond was instantly forged in that small room of triumph.

Sophia was so weak or too sad even to smile. She just held her baby, tears streaming quietly down her eyes as the baby's cries filled the room. Watching them, I wanted to cry, too. I suddenly remembered that Ciaran was in the room. I glanced at him, curious about what he had planned next. He had a slight smile plastered to his face as he stared intently at the baby. He looked relieved.

"Well, now. Congratulations," he said. He began to walk towards Sophia and her baby. I got up and stood in his way.

"Don't come any closer," I said firmly.

"Or what?" Ciaran asked calmly, a devious smile spreading across his lips. "You cannot stop me. Especially not in your state."

"I can try. I wouldn't underestimate me if I were you," I smirked, hoping that would intimidate him a little.

"Oh, I never underestimate anyone," he said. "Certainly not you."

He waved his hand, and the next thing I knew, I flew through the air and across the room. I hit my head against the wall and fell to the floor hard while Ciaran approached Sophia. I groaned as I pulled myself up again and leaped into Ciaran's chest. He was shocked that I could still use that much of my power. I sent him flying almost halfway across the room, falling short of hitting the wall. By the time he got up, his smile had disappeared, replaced by anger and malice.

I scoffed. I was breaking through the hold this collar had on me with all the strength I could summon. I knew my wolf had to be on the other end, helping us get free from this resistance. He was not getting to Sophia and her baby.

"I'm starting to understand what Warwick meant when he said you are a huge pain in the ass." Before I could say anything, he raised a hand and caught me in his telekinetic field, lifting me off the ground. "But you have no idea who you are dealing with, child."

Child? He looked like he was in the same age group as me.

It felt like there was an invisible hand holding me up by the neck, and I was struggling with the invisible hand. It looked like Ciaran was ready to strangle me to death. He had no reason not to kill me now. I had done my part. I had delivered Sophia's baby. *Was I about to die?*

I remember a forbidden magic my mother told me about. Centuries ago, during the persecution of witches, men discovered ways to test whether one was a witch or not. After many witches were caught and killed, some who were left came together to figure out how to evade their enemies. A spell to make them fail the test of witches. Passing the test would mean one was a witch.

The test was as practical as it was crude. A drop of blood was all that was required. The blood was boiled in water, and some additives were mixed in with it. The results showed the percentage of constituents in the blood. A witch's blood was said to be high in a particular element that, till now, had not been given a name. It appeared that element made us different from the rest of humankind. So, the key to failing the witch test was finding how to hide that element. Well, nothing some magic couldn't fix. That was every witch's slogan from the beginning of time.

After much research and trial, the witches found a spell that would help hide their identity. The spell was classified under the forbidden magics because it required a witch to incur harm upon themselves. Bone for bone. Blood for blood. When the spell was being cast, a witch must deliberately break a bone in their body and immediately spill their blood. This way, the element showing off its magic is dried up temporarily. During this period, the witch's use of magic was usually severely limited.

However, another group — of non-human-like beings — held an insurmountable amount of power that, if my kind could tap into that power, would bring us back from extinction. But these beings blended so well with everyone that it wasn't easy to ascertain who they were or how to locate them. Some were lucky to find these beings and could dabble in the forbidden magics, but it came at a significant cost.

Somehow, I believed the collar around my neck was created by one of those beings, and the magic used on it was forbidden. If Ciaran was one of those beings, I was in trouble.

If I were to break the collar's effect—this was a huge gamble—the same procedure might hold as it did in the past. Perhaps if I break my bone and shed some blood, I could get a window of opportunity to use my magic and break the collar. And that was what I would do before Sophia's unprecedented delivery.

And now, at the precipice of death, it looked like it might be my only option. Without thinking, I grabbed one of my fingers and twisted it painfully backward. I let out a shout. But I didn't stop. My ring had a small nail I could expose whenever I needed to get a little bloody during a fight. I jabbed the nail into my palm and dragged it down, tearing the middle of my palm open.

"What the hell are you doing?" Ciaran asked.

My blood began to pour down. I shut my eyes tightly for a moment, praying that this worked. When I opened my eyes, I said a word of spell. At once, Ciaran's telekinetic hold on me broke, and I fell to the ground.

"Fuck!" I groaned in pain. I immediately pulled myself back up and tried my hand on the collar again. My wolf strength was also back. I ripped the collar off without effect. Ciaran could not believe his eyes. Neither could Sophia.

Hell, neither could I.

It actually worked. I thought I was losing my mind.

Focus.

It was me against Ciaran fair and square now. Magic versus magic. Let's see just how powerful he was.

I picked a chair close to the bed and threw it at him, and I immediately picked the bedside table close by and hurtled that at him, too. I was able to fling the table with my wolf strength easily. Ciaran had waved the chair away, but was too distracted watching the table come at him to see me lunge. I landed a blow on his face with my fist, sending him crashing into the window nearby. He fell and blood began running down the side of his face.

He raised a hand toward me and muttered a few words in his foreign language. The spell held me locked in place. I couldn't move an inch. I struggled to free myself, but his hold was too strong. As he got up and walked towards me, a pair of scissors pierced through the air and embedded itself in the side of his arm. He shouted in pain. I looked over to find out it was Sophia who threw them. I wondered where she got the scissors or how the hell she knew how to throw like that. But she distracted Ciaran long enough to have his hold on me soften, and then I returned the spell on him, locking him in place.

Just then, I heard a sound behind me. Everything was happening too fast. My consciousness was beginning to fade as I used too much stored energy. I turned back to find Warwick with a claw pressed to Sophia's neck while she was still holding her baby, who was now crying so loudly that my ears throbbed.

"Look how beautiful my pup is," Warwick said with a grin. "Stand down, Kara. Or Sophia here gets it."

I needed help. I could no longer do this on my own. Now that I had my powers back, I would attempt reaching John.

14

John

Three days had passed, and we still hadn't found Kara. I knew she was still alive. I could feel her. I could also sense her calling out for me to save her. My wolf stirred as it was an uneasy feeling not being able to save my mate. Aiden was the only one who could reach me telepathically. It had to be Kara's powers as a witch. If she was calling out to me in this manner, she had to be in serious trouble.

I adjusted my grip on the phone as I dialed Vince's number. I was done waiting. I needed to know what his decision was, so I knew what my next step would be. I had been mentally preparing myself to be the alpha of this pack a little longer, should Vince refuse to take the role.

The familiar ringtone echoed in my ear as I waited for him to pick up. Finally, after what felt like an eternity, his voice crackled through the line.

"Hey, cousin. What's up?" Vince's voice carried a hint of weariness as if he had been contemplating something important before my call interrupted his thoughts.

"Hey, Vince. Listen, I think it's about time we talked," I replied, my voice laced with urgency. "I need to know what your decision is. Aiden must have told you about how he wants you to take up the role of pack master here in New York, a position I'm temporarily occupying. But I am about to make some moves, and I need to know if you will be here or not."

There was a brief pause on the other end, and I imagined Vince's eyebrows furrowing as he processed my words. "I've never really considered it before, but I've been thinking about it a lot lately. Frankly, I am a little surprised that Aiden would trust me with this responsibility. I know he loves me. And I love him, too."

A wave of relief washed over me as I heard his words. It seemed like Vince was truly considering the weight of the responsibility that came with being an alpha. "That's great, Vince. We need someone like you to step up and take charge. The pack needs a strong leader."

Vince let out a deep sigh, his voice filled with a mix of determination and resignation. "You know, cuz, my days as a lone wolf have been filled with adventures and freedom. But I've come to realize that it's time for me to take responsibility and settle down. I've had enough of the wandering life. I'm ready to embrace this role."

A surge of pride swelled within me as I listened to Vince's words. He had always been fiercely independent, so hearing him speak of putting down roots was a sign of growth and maturity. Was he ready to find his mate and raise a family of his own?

"I'm glad to hear that, Vince. You have what it takes to lead this pack with strength and compassion. So, when are you coming?" I asked, eager to have Vince here. Ready for him to embark on this new chapter.

There was a sense of determination in Vince's voice as he responded, "Very soon, John. I've been making the necessary arrangements, and I'll be there before you know it. I'm ready to embrace this role and join the pack."

A smile tugged at the corners of my lips as I imagined the impact Vince's arrival would have on the pack. With his experience in being around other packs around the nation and his newfound dedication, I knew he would bring them together and guide them toward a prosperous future.

"That's great, Vince. You have no idea how happy I am about this. A lot is going on, cousin." I sighed. "I need you here real soon. I need your tracking skills and your muscles."

I didn't want to involve him before, but I am left with no choice. He was my last resort and he needed to know what he was getting himself into. Vince was the greatest tracker I knew amongst our kind. It was probably because he had spent so long on his own honing his skills to the fullest.

Vince's curiosity seemed to be piqued. His voice carried a mixture of concern and intrigue as he probed further, wanting to understand the urgency behind my request.

"What's going on, John? Why do you need my tracking skills? Is something wrong?"

Taking a deep breath, I hesitated for a moment, unsure of how much to reveal. But I trusted Vince, and I knew he deserved to know the truth.

"Vince, a woman has been kidnapped by a rogue wolf. He was banished from this pack. She's important to me, and I need your help to find her."

There was a brief pause on the other end, and I could almost envision Vince's furrowed brow as he processed my words. His voice softened. I had a feeling he was trying to read my thoughts and complete the blanks in my statements even over the phone.

"Important, huh? In what way, John?"

I swallowed the lump in my throat, my voice tinged with vulnerability. "She might be my mate, Vince. I can't explain it fully, but there's a connection between us. I can't bear the thought of losing her to those rogue wolves."

Silence hung in the air for a moment, broken only by the distant sounds of the city in the background on the phone. I was curious about where he was staying currently. I could almost hear Vince's mind working, piecing together the significance of my words. His voice, when it finally came, was laced with a newfound understanding.

"Your mate, John? That changes things. I can sense the weight of this situation now. I'll do whatever it takes to find her and bring her back safely."

"There was another woman, Sophia, who was also taken and she's pregnant."

"I'll be there as soon as I can, cousin," he said.

Relief washed over me as I heard the determination in Vince's voice. He understood the gravity of the situation and was committed to helping me rescue the woman who held such importance in my heart, along with Sophia, who I knew was in as much grave danger as Kara. I hoped that she and her unborn child were okay.

"Thank you, Vince," I said, gratitude lacing my words. "Your support means the world to me. Together, we'll find them and bring them back home."

I ended the call. Now that I knew Vince was coming, I knew things were bound to get really interesting.

My mind went to a call I received the previous night. I'd been alpha for barely a week and so much had happened already. I'd met with a strong hybrid one-on-one, and I'd had to experience what it was like to finally meet my mate, more or less. I also had to deal with rogue wolves and those who were not overly happy to have an Omega standing in as their alpha. I was feeling the weight of it all pressing down on me. Now, I was having to deal with an alpha of a particular breed I had no intention of pissing off.

Paul walked in, stopped in front of the desk, and crossed his arms. He was right on time.

"Hey, Paul. Glad you could make it," I said. I gestured for him to take a seat, and as he settled across from me, I prepared to share the news that had come my way.

"Sure thing, boss man," he replied.

"Paul, I received a message from the alpha of a dragon hoard. He reached out to me, informing me that there's a wolf causing trouble within his territory," I explained.

We shared this part of New York with the dragons and other shifters, so we were basically neighbors. But we had clear boundaries and territories. Dragons and wolves were not enemies, but we were not on the best of terms either. We tried to stay away from each other's paths, and we tried not to cross our various boundaries unless it was absolutely necessary.

Paul's brow furrowed, a flicker of recognition crossing his features. "Let me guess, it's Warwick, right?" His tone held disappointment as if he had anticipated this revelation. "Please tell me it is."

I nodded. "Yes, it is. The alpha of the dragon hoard mentioned that Warwick has been going to their bar and hitting on his girlfriend, causing trouble. I asked how he knew who he was, and he said that Warwick introduced himself, saying he was from our pack, and that I was his pack master."

A deep sigh escaped my lips as I shook my head, mirroring Paul's disappointment.

"I can't believe Warwick would stoop this low. It's disheartening to see one of our own causing such trouble," Paul said.

"I agree. Warwick's actions reflect poorly not just on our entire pack, but our kind. It's disappointing to witness his reckless behavior." Warwick had grown brave, but also reckless. Suddenly, I remembered Seth. I didn't let Paul know that I was in touch with him. I should probably tell him soon, for my safety in case Seth decided to make some funny moves on me in order to seal his role as alpha. He did offer to help, but would he help track Warwick?

"We can't let this slide, John. It's time to confront Warwick and remind him of his responsibilities as a member of our pack," Paul said, then he paused as a realization hit him. "Wait, you banished him, along with that Seth guy, didn't you? We should be able to wreak judgment on him now that he is an outlaw in the wolf community."

Paul was suggesting that we kill Warwick. I had a feeling it might result to that eventually, but I didn't want us to get ahead of ourselves. He needed to be turned in for his crimes. The FBI was still looking for him, which meant that I needed to call Phillip and inform him of Warwick's whereabouts. However, I wanted to bust down Warwick's door myself. Phillip and the FBI could wait until after we've rescued Kara and Sophia.

My eyes narrowed. "You're absolutely right, Paul. We need to hold Warwick accountable for his actions. We can't allow him to tarnish this pack's reputation any longer. The council would want us to turn him over to them, I'm sure. I need to speak with the alpha of the dragon hoard again and get as much detail as I can. He might be able to help us locate Warwick."

"I guess you're right," Paul said. "I'll go with you. I don't think walking into dragon territory alone is a good idea."

"Don't worry about me, Paul. You just maintain the order here. I will be fine."

Paul squinted his eyes, and then he swallowed his breath. He knew that I could take care of myself. And that was the truth. As he got up to leave, I broke the news about Vince to him.

"He said he's taking the role," I said.

Paul remained quiet for a minute before nodding his head. "That's great," he said. "Looking forward to seeing him again. It's been too long." With that, he walked out of the office.

I got up, preparing to go meet with the alpha of the dragon hoard. I think he mentioned that his name was Mason. I had already arranged a meeting with him over the call last night. The truth was I wasn't meeting him alone. I was going with Seth. I had been dancing with fire since I stepped foot onto this territory and assumed the role of alpha of a pack. I hope I didn't get burnt soon. Before I went, I needed to make one more phone call.

15

John

I stood in front of the bar, my eyes scanning the bustling crowd that spilled onto the sidewalk. The neon sign above the entrance flickered, casting an ethereal glow on the faces of those who entered and exited. Of course, I should expect a wolf like Seth to come late for a meeting. I was angry when I saw him slip out of an alleyway across the street. I was taking a gamble in asking him to join me.

After I got off the phone with Mason, I called Seth to ask if he wanted to join me tonight. I was putting a lot of faith in trusting him to be honest with me. He was supposed to be banished however, after careful consideration, he may have been in the wrong place at the wrong time. I made the decision to give him another chance to prove himself.

Seth's eyes darted around as he approached me as if he didn't want to get seen. I wouldn't blame him if he was nervous. I was. Two wolves walk into a bar full of dragons. There had to be a punch line in there somewhere. *Deep breaths.*

I cleared my throat, pushing my anxiety back down. "Remember, Seth, let me do the talking. We need to handle this situation delicately."

Seth nodded. His hands were tucked in the pocket of his jacket. I was well aware he tended to show me that he was worthy enough to be allowed to stay. He seemed as if he was a level-headed guy. I needed him to keep his cool, or else this meeting might turn out for the worse. Looking at how shifty he was, dusting his nose every second, or constantly running his fingers through his hair, I was having second thoughts. Bringing him along was probably a terrible idea.

"Nervous?" I asked him with raised eyebrows.

"Very. Have you any idea where we are?" he asked with wide eyes.

"Yes, I do. We needed to meet on their turf as a sign of goodwill and to earn their trust." I drew in a deep breath and released it loudly through my nose. "Look, I need you to calm down. I can't have you going in there looking like a nervous wreck right now. I'm sure they can smell you all the way out here."

With another deep breath, I pushed open the heavy wooden doors of the bar, and we stepped inside. The atmosphere instantly enveloped us, buzzing with an exhilarating and intimidating energy. The bar was dimly lit, the warm glow of overhead lights casting an amber hue over the room.

As my eyes adjusted to the dimness, I was greeted by a sight I had never seen before — a multitude of dragons, yet in human form. They filled the bar, their presence both majestic and awe-inspiring. Some were sitting on barstools, blending seamlessly with the surrounding furniture. Others stood tall, their eyes gleaming with a mix of curiosity and territoriality.

I could sense the magic in how they hid their true form from being seen. It was like an optical allusion. I could see their wings folded neatly against their backs if I focused long enough. I tried not to stare too long, but it was hard not to. Some of them had unique colored hair that I was told ages ago represented the color of their dragon-self, and I tried to picture each one in their dragon form. I had never seen one before, yet I wasn't sure if I genuinely wanted to.

My wolf was on guard, ready at a moment's notice if I had to shift. I would probably be shredded before I had the chance to shift completely. That thought alone had my anxiety coming up to the surface.

The air was thick with the scent of smoke and the sound of rumbling conversations. The dragons conversed in low voices, their words carrying an otherworldly resonance as they spoke a language unknown to me. The room seemed to vibrate with their presence, a powerful energy that sent shivers down my spine.

I glanced at Seth, his eyes wide with wonder. The sheer number of dragons was overwhelming, even for me, but I knew we had a purpose here. Taking a moment to steady myself, I approached the bar, navigating through the crowd with Seth trailing closely behind.

As we found a spot by the counter, I noticed a few dragons in their complete dragon form, their massive bodies curled and coiled, taking up considerable space. It was a sight that filled me with trepidation and respect. I had heard tales of such transformations, but to witness it firsthand was a humbling experience.

The bartender, a human who seemed unfazed by the presence of these mythical creatures, approached us. I leaned in, my voice low but assertive. "We're here to speak with the alpha of the dragon hoard. He's expecting me. Can you point us in the right direction?"

The bartender nodded, gesturing towards a secluded corner of the bar where a man sat regally. "He's over there. Good luck."

With a nod of gratitude, I led the way, Seth following closely. As we approached the alpha, I couldn't help but marvel at the extraordinary world that had opened before us. The bar teemed with dragons, their power and majesty evident in every corner. The bar itself was a marvel to behold as it appeared much bigger on the inside than it did from the parking lot.

Mason, the alpha of the dragon hoard, sat in a secluded corner of the bar, his presence commanding the attention of those around him. I approached him, my eyes taking in his formidable figure. Mason's long, flowing golden hair cascaded down his broad shoulders, adding an air of regality to his appearance. His sturdy build and tall structure exuded a quiet strength that demanded respect. He had features that reminded me of a Norseman, and I wondered if he may be from that region.

As I drew closer, I couldn't help but notice the beautiful woman at his side, her radiant presence accentuating Mason's allure. Her flowing locks, the color of fiery embers, framed her delicate features, and her enchanting eyes sparkled with warmth and confidence. It was evident why Mason would be fiercely protective of her, given her undeniable beauty and the allure it held for others.

Mason's sharp gaze met mine, and he nodded at his mate, signaling her to excuse herself. She gracefully stood, casting a brief smile in my direction before approaching the bar, leaving Mason and me to converse in private.

I took a moment to gather my thoughts, impressed by Mason's commanding presence. His aura exuded a combination of authority and wisdom, leaving no doubt as to why he held the position of alpha. I approached him warily, mindful of the delicate situation at hand.

"I try my best not to cause trouble for the wolves in these parts," he said. In person, he sounded more — elderly, like he was much older than he looked, which was entirely possible because dragons lived far longer than wolves. For what it was worth, he could be over five centuries old. "And I keep my hoard in check, too. I'm a man of peace. So, imagine my surprise when one of you begins to start a war with us."

"I can see you are angry. I…"

He raised his hand, signaling for me to be silent as he wasn't done talking. I gave a little nod, letting him continue.

"Your wolf tried to force my mate into his car right here in front of the bar. You are lucky I'm not quick to spill fire. I hear it is not his first time having a go at my mate. You should get your wolf in check, or I will check him for you. And rest assured, more wolves other than him will get hurt when I do that."

"Thank you for your patience. I'll deal with it. Warwick is a wolf that has been banished from our pack. He is nothing but trouble. We've been looking for him. Perhaps you could help. Maybe tell me where last you saw him. I know you must have kept an eye on him since he began to give you trouble."

I felt Warwick was trying to cause trouble for me and his former pack as a selfish way to get back at us. He wasn't satisfied with me pushing him out of the alpha standing. I don't understand why he would make such a dangerous move targeting another alpha's mate, though. Perhaps he didn't know who she was. Either way, he needs to be stopped.

Mason scribbled on a napkin and handed it to me. He stared at Seth hard and frowned. "I don't like this one," he said, his stare lingering on Seth, who was almost growling.

I stole a look at the napkin before tucking it into my pocket. It contained an address. "Okay, thank you so much, Mason. We will be on our way now. I can assure you, Warwick won't be disturbing any of you again. Come on, Seth."

I got up to leave. Seth took his time to get up. He was scowling at Mason as if he would put up a fight. I was sure Seth was strong, but there was no way he was stupid enough to think he could take the alpha of a dragon hoard in his own place.

"Seth," I called him again. This time, he turned and walked past me. I smiled at Mason. "I do apologize for Seth."

"You apologize a lot for an alpha," he smirked.

Not knowing what to say to that, I nodded and left.

16

John

As soon as we exited the bar, I turned toward Seth and asked, "What is wrong with you?"

He grinned as if he knew what I was asking, but instead, he asked, "What do you mean?"

"You know what I mean. Challenging an alpha dragon. Are you mad?" I said a little quietly so as not to stir any dragons nearby.

I wasn't sure if they were listening in. I'm sure that they were. We weren't but a few feet away from the door. Any of them could come outside, and there could be chaos afterward. I didn't want that to happen. I needed an alliance with this hoard, at least for Vince's sake.

"I am putting a lot on the line giving you a second chance in staying with this pack. You aren't helping yourself any."

Seth scoffed and then put his hand out, "Give me the address he gave you, John."

I suddenly didn't feel like sharing the information with him. They say dragons could smell intentions from afar. The same could be said about Omegas. I should've gone with my instincts not to trust Seth, and I was an idiot to have him join me instead of Paul.

I turned on my heel and headed for my car, with Seth following close behind. I glanced down at the napkin, memorizing the address, and pushed the napkin deep into my jeans pocket again.

"John, tell me the address," Seth asked again when I didn't respond. I could hear the threat underneath his words.

I spun around, stopping him in his tracks, and asked sharply, "What do you want with it?"

"It's none of your business," he said arrogantly.

"Except it is. I'm trying to save two women and an unborn pup."

"And I'm trying to bring Warwick down. Our goals align."

"What are you going to do with him?" I asked.

I could sense he wasn't being truthful and omitting information. Had he aligned himself with Warwick and needed to warn him? Indeed, Warwick would've told Seth where he was. Maybe Seth had a sudden change of plans and wanted to join him. He wasn't getting this address.

Ignoring my question, he huffed, "Give me the address, John."

"No," I said sternly, taking a step forward. It was a challenging move that I unknowingly took, but I would stand firm on my answer. He was not going to jeopardize this rescue mission. Warwick needed to pay, that was certain, but after talking to the Council last night, they needed me to turn him over for sentencing.

Seth growled at me, splaying his canines and taking a stance of attack.

I ignored him, hoping he would back down. Deep down, I knew he wouldn't, and my wolf was already on edge. "Warwick will be dealt with the proper way. My way, given that I am the alpha," I lied. "Stand down, Seth."

"You're no alpha," he growled and then charged.

Shit. I growled, my fangs coming out, too, and I braced myself for impact. He quickly swept me off my feet. In no time, he was on top of me and was about to slice my neck with his claws when something shoved him away before he could do that. It was another wolf. I wasn't sure if it was any wolf from the New York pack, but I recognized it somehow. The parking lot wasn't well-lit, but I could only see a giant wolf with a dark coat. My eyes glanced down and saw the milky white tips, and I shook my head, astonished by what he showed.

"Vince?" I muttered.

He shifted back into human form but didn't let Seth out of sight. "I could smell you from a hundred miles away, cousin. You still smell like shit," Vince chuckled.

I laughed, feeling elated to see him. "Vince!"

"Who the hell are you?" Seth asked, dusting himself off as he got up. He could barely stand straight. I knew Vince had to have hit him quite hard.

I got to my feet, too, feeling shaky from the adrenalin rush. "Seth, this is the one I was standing in for. This is the real alpha of the pack. Your pack master."

"I'm guessing this is one of the troublesome wolves," Vince said. Seth took a step back, and rightfully so. Vince was slightly taller than Seth and possibly more muscular. As kids, Vince, Aiden, and I would wrestle around. Vince and Aiden took it easy on me as I was the smallest of the three. However, when Vince and Aiden wrestled, Vince would win most of the time.

"I'll take care of things from here." Vince gave a smirk that made Seth swallow audibly. "You're going to go back home." His voice was so commanding that I almost walked to my car to go back home.

For the first time, I noticed that Vince was not alone. We were so preoccupied with Seth that I didn't see that Vince had a young woman with him. She maintained a reasonable distance from us, and probably for good reasons.

Vince turned his attention to me and saw me staring. He smiled. "Oh, that's my mate," he said. "Her name is Lissa. She came here in search of her sister. She only recently found out she had a sister. You wouldn't happen to know a Kara, would you?"

My eyes widened. Kara had a sister.

"Uh, yeah. That's who I was hoping you would help me track."

Vince cocked his head back, his eyebrows furrowed in confusion. "Hold on, Kara is your mate?" I nodded, and Vince laughed softly as he walked over and helped me to my feet. "We have a lot of catching up to do."

I glanced over at Lissa, who was staring at me with wide eyes, and said, "Apparently."

I couldn't believe he even said 'my mate' when introducing her. I was not only stunned but happy for them both. It was about time that he finally settled down. Lissa had flaming red hair and a fair complexion. She was gorgeous; if I had scented her correctly, she was also a dragon. That was even more surprising.

Without another word, Seth left us. Vince walked over to me and wrapped his arms around me in a tight hug. "Man, it's good to see you again, cuz," he said. He stepped back and asked, "Where do we need to start?"

I was glad he was ready to get going. "I have Warwick's address. I'm unsure if he's keeping Kara and Sophia there."

"It's a start. Let's go."

17

John

When we arrived at the address Mason had given me, a few dragons were waiting outside the house as if they were acting as the lookout. They stepped out of their car the moment we did. One of them approached us, while the others stayed behind and watched us, albeit cautiously. I could sense that Vince was on high alert with their appearance.

"I forgot to mention that I had met with the alpha of the dragon hoard today."

"That would've been helpful on our drive over here," Vince chuckled. He rolled his shoulders and drew in a deep breath, releasing it through his nose, and I could sense his anxiety slowly dropping.

"The male wolf is still inside, but the human male has left," the dragon said. "Not sure when or if he's going to return."

"Thank you for sharing that bit of information," I replied with a small smile. "Are you here to help?"

It was a question I need an answer to. Were they here to help or watch? Though I was sure Vince could take care of Warwick, it wouldn't hurt to have help if things got out of hand. I didn't want anything to happen to Sophia or Kara, let alone Vince and I or his mate.

The dragon's lips broke out in a smile that had my hair standing on end and my wolf on edge. His eyes flickered, changing colors, and he barred his elongating fangs. I knew he was close to changing, but he didn't shift, and I was thankful for that.

"Mason sent us here to help. We want to ensure things go smoothly and this wolf is removed from our town."

"He's to be taken into custody. The Council is expecting him in one piece, if possible. He's also a person of interest to the FBI. Their agent, a wolf named Phillip, is on his way. I gave him a call after I left your place."

"You better hope that he chooses to remain in one piece. I have orders from my alpha to intervene should it require it."

"Understood," Vince replied and nodded at me to silently say that he was ready to go.

Vince kicked the door in, and we found Warwick on the couch in the living room. He must've been asleep as his reaction was slow. I quickly bypassed him, leaving Vince to take care of him, and headed down the hallway. I could smell Kara's scent strongly there. My heart leaped in my chest. She was here.

"In here," Kara called out. Her voice was muffled but close by.

I followed her voice to the room at the end of the hallway. My heart lurched into my throat the moment I opened the door and saw her chained to the bed. Sophia was sitting up, clutching what I believed to be her newborn child in a blanket to her chest.

"Is everyone all right?" I asked, my gaze finding Kara's face again.

Tears trailed down her cheeks, and I could feel a sense of joy and relief emanating from her. I knelt before her to assess the chain situation when she leaped into my arms, nearly knocking me over. My arms immediately went around her, and I held her against my chest. My wolf sighed a sense of relief, and we had our mate safe in our embrace.

The baby in Sophia's arms began to stir fussily as the sounds coming from the living room grew louder. Warwick was not going to go quietly. From the growls, nips, and sounds of shredded and broken things, I ascertained that they had shifted and were now fighting one another. Was it a fight for life or dominance? I wasn't sure. One thing was certain: I needed to get Kara, Sophia, and her newborn out of here to safety.

As if she could read my mind, "I'm unsure who has the key. Ciaran was the last one in here. Warwick had him chain me back up so I didn't get any ideas about trying to escape again."

Again? My heart broke hearing her say those words. I was kicking myself for not being able to get here sooner.

"I'll find it," I said to her, then turned my attention to Sophia. "Are you two okay?"

"Yes," she replied, her voice coming out shaky.

"I know you're scared. Try to ignore what's going on in the other room. My cousin Vince is taking care of Warwick. We're getting you all out of here. Baby included."

"Thank you," she replied, wiping the tears from her cheek with the back of her hand.

"I have some friends who are outside waiting for us. Do you think I can help you get outside?" I asked Sophia, and she nodded. "Vince's mate is in the car, and she can sit with you until I can get Kara free from this chain."

I helped her off the bed and led her to the door. I heard a yip and a thud when I opened the door. Ignoring Sophia, I rushed to the living room to see Vince changing back into his human form before kneeling over Warwick and checking his pulse.

"He's still alive," Vince panted, sitting back on his heels. "But just barely." Blood oozed from a cut above his eyebrow and dripped down his face. He dug. Through a pile of shredded clothes, and frowned as if what he found amongst them couldn't be salvaged.

"Are you okay?" I asked, feeling genuinely concerned for my cousin's well-being.

He nodded, but suddenly, he reached his hand out and grabbed onto the couch beside him as he swayed over to his left, catching himself from falling over onto the floor. "Just a little woozy," he mumbled. "It'll pass."

Understanding it may be a bit of low blood sugar. I rushed into the kitchen to find something to help. I could only find a bottle of water, half a loaf of bread, and a pop tart. "Pop tart and water it is," I muttered. I quickly returned to my cousin and handed him the food I found. "I need to check Warwick's pants for some keys. Kara is chained to the bed. Sophia and the baby appear to be okay."

Vince's lip curled into a snarl. His eyes darted to Warwick, who was still unmoving on the ground. "You're so lucky that the Council wants you. I would be more than happy to finish you off myself."

"I could hold off calling them."

"And risk getting into trouble? No thanks. He's not worth it. Besides, I'm sure the Council needs to make an example out of him. If I were to call saying they missed the opportunity, I may be his replacement."

He stood up and took a bite of his food as his eyes roamed the living room, searching for something in particular. I fumbled through the pile of clothes in search of keys.

The front door flew open, and Vince and I jumped to our feet, ready to pounce, when Mason rushed inside with two of his dragons. He stopped within a few feet of us, his body relaxing after taking in the scenery. Warwick was still out when Vince had found some duct tape and wrapped it around Warwick's arms and legs.

"Forgive me for barging in," Mason drawled. "It was a little too quiet for my tastes. I needed to check that you wolves were okay and got what you came for."

"Thanks for checking up on us, Mason," Vince said as he finished the last bite of his pop tart.

I turned my head in Vince's direction with a surprised expression on my face. "How do you know Mason?"

Vince smirked, "He helped me out with a similar situation. It seems that the human Warwick was working with may be more trouble than you were aware."

Mason drew in a deep breath and released it with a loud sigh through his nose. "Ciaran is a bit of a problem in our world, as well as the human's world, and needs to be stopped. He's a powerful druid, so he's been hard to locate."

"I see," I replied. "It would've helped to know all this."

"We'll track Ciaran down eventually and deal with him," Mason replied.

"Hopefully, before he does this again," Vince added.

"I feel like I'm missing something," I said.

"I'm not sure how much Warwick and Ciaran were working together, but they may have been part of an organization kidnapping women."

"Especially if they are a rare species," Mason added. "Kelpies, dragons, Fae, and even your wolf mate are catches for anyone with the money to buy them. The list of who they want is quite long."

"My mate, Lissa, is a dragon shifter. She told me that they had kidnapped a few other unique individuals along with her in hopes of selling them to breed," Vince added. "It's disgusting."

"It is and needs to be shut down," I added. I hated that my cousin had to endure what I dealt with. What was happening was disgusting, and it needed to be stopped.

Mason nodded. "I agree. We've been working with the Council to locate as many of those behind this as possible. Catching Ciaran is crucial as we believe he's much higher up in the chain of command than we think."

I needed to free Kara from the confines of that chain and her room and finish talking to Vince and Mason. I'm sure that once Kara was free, Vince would be the alpha, and this matter would no longer be my concern, but it was whoever was out there taking our kind with ill intentions needed to pay. Was the Council aware of what was going on? I'm not sure. Now that I had more information, they needed to know. Though that was not my job anymore, as it fell onto Vince's shoulders, it still wouldn't hurt to pass the word along. If not, let Aiden know.

18

John

I was jet lagged and feeling it, but my brother and I had a lot of catching up to do. He said he had great news that he couldn't wait to tell me.

"Twins?" I replied, my voice a little higher. I was extremely happy for my brother and his mate for all they have gone through. They both deserved this.

"I know. I couldn't believe it myself, but we're having twins," Aiden said with a huge grin.

"How's Gemma doing?" I asked. It felt like an eternity since I had seen her, even though I had been gone a few weeks.

"She's doing great. Glowing and as surprised and excited as I am," he beamed.

Aiden was overjoyed, and understandably so. I stared at my brother across his desk, and my mind wandered back to Kara. I hoped that she was doing well. A small part of me hoped she would change her mind and accept me as her mate. Would I be sitting across from my brother, reveling in the glow of fatherhood as he was? Time will only tell.

Vince took over the pack as alpha without trouble, but Paul and I stayed for several days to ensure all went well. Mostly, I stayed because I wanted to spend some time with Kara. She seemed interested in us getting to know one another, but she also felt she needed time before moving forward in a relationship.

Maybe it was what she had gone through or the fact that she had never had a real relationship. I wanted to be there with her to show her that I was there for her, but she insisted that I return home and give her some time to think.

My wolf had been quiet since leaving New York, and I was afraid it was because Kara didn't come back with us. I wanted to give her space and the freedom to choose, even if her choice was painful. She said she needed time, and I could only give her all of it that she needed by walking away.

The moment I stepped onto my flight back home, my chest began to ache. I had only heard stories of those whose mating bond was not accepted. It was a fate worse than moon sickness. I now knew what my brother was suffering through all those months ago. Paul had stayed behind, having spent his time looking after Sophia and her daughter. I fought to keep it together the whole flight home. But now, sitting with my brother and hearing him talk about family helped chip away at that final piece that was holding me together.

"Hey, brother," Aiden said softly. I didn't see him stand up, walk around his desk, and approach my chair. Tears stung my eyes, threatening to fall as I peered up at him. "She'll come around," he said with a small smile.

I nodded. I wanted to believe him. I hated showing this side of myself. I was the one who helped others in our pack when they were feeling down, and now, I feel like I am the one who needs help.

A stray tear finally fell, and I turned toward the photos on the wall behind his desk. It was covered with pictures of our pack and our family. When we arrived, I told Aiden how everything went, but he sensed that I was leaving something out. I told him everything, leaving nothing out, including Kara being my mate.

My mind wandered back to when Vince and I rescued Kara and Sophia. They were safe and that was all that mattered. I needed to focus on getting back to work now that I was home. Though, it didn't feel much like home to me as I felt like I left a part of it in New York.

19

Kara

I stood at the edge of the small lake, enveloped in the serenity of the moment. The rippling water reflected the golden hues of the setting sun, casting a warm glow over the surrounding landscape. Breathing in the crisp autumn air, I allowed myself to bask in the tranquility, my mind wandering back to the recent events that had unfolded.

Vince and John had saved Sophia and me from Warwick. The memory still sent shivers down my spine. I knew John would come for me. The night before our rescue, I had a vision he would. The moment he stormed into the house, he made me feel overjoyed.

My wolf stirred as I remembered him rushing into the room where Sophia and I were staying. Tears stung my eyes, threatening to fall. He was my literal knight in shining armor. Ciaran, the enigmatic witch aiding Warwick, had managed to escape during the chaos. I couldn't help but wonder whether he had achieved whatever mysterious goal he sought from Warwick.

A torrent of mixed emotions flooded my thoughts as I gazed out over the peaceful lake. I pondered the fate that awaited Warwick, the man who had inflicted so much pain upon us. Would he face a punishment befitting his malevolence? Vince had assured me that Warwick would never trouble us again, but the uncertainty lingered in my mind. Would the Council go as far as to end his life or sentence him in some specially made prison for our kind? The thought sent a chill down my spine, but strangely, I was indifferent to his fate.

Sophia and her daughter were safe. That was all that mattered. She wasn't sure if she wanted to stay with the pack, no matter how much Vince had assured her of their safety. She needed time to think it over. In the meantime, she was going to stay at my sanctuary.

Warwick had shattered my sense of security and violated the sanctuary of my life. He had caused significant damage. The mere thought of him being set free, capable of perpetrating more harm, filled me with seething anger. I yearned for justice. However, it may manifest.

Amid my contemplation, the wind whispered through the trees, carrying away my doubts and fears. The beauty of the surrounding nature, untouched by the darkness that had plagued us, served as a reminder of the resilience of life itself.

The gentle breeze caressed my face as I stood by the edge of the tranquil lake, carrying memories that stirred my heart. One memory stood out vividly: I met Lissa, my long-lost sister. The revelation had left me utterly stunned, for I had never known of her existence until that fateful day.

I recollected the peculiar circumstances surrounding our encounter. It was during one of my debilitating visions when I first glimpsed Lissa in a trance-like state. Her face, foreign, appeared before me, and an inexplicable connection resonated between us. At the time, I couldn't comprehend the significance of her presence, but little did I know that she would soon walk into my life, unveiling a newfound sense of belonging.

Realizing that I had a sister, a blood relative, was overwhelming and surreal. For years, I had navigated life's challenges alone, devoid of any familial ties aside from my mother, but she had left me when I was young. Her absence had left an indelible void within me that I had unknowingly yearned to fill. At that moment, as Lissa stepped into my life, I felt that void began to mend.

The joy and happiness that welled up within me were immeasurable. I couldn't help but cherish the prospect of having an actual family once more, someone who shared my bloodline and understood the depths of my journey. Lissa brought the promise of shared laughter, tears, and memories. It was a chance to build a bond that would withstand the test of time, anchoring us to each other through the tumultuous seas of life.

A renewed sense of gratitude washed over me as I reminisced by the lake's edge. Lissa's arrival had breathed new life into my world, rekindling the flickering flame of hope that had dimmed over the years. Though uncertainty lingered regarding the true meaning behind her sudden appearance, I cast aside any doubts, embracing the warmth of love and companionship that now enveloped me.

With each passing day, as we unraveled the intricacies of our shared history, I marveled at the beauty of this unexpected reunion. In the quiet solitude of the lake's embrace, I allowed myself a moment of peaceful contentment.

My gaze shifted towards John, and my heart fluttered with affection. A smile tugged at my lips, mirroring the one that graced his face when he saw me in that room with Sophia. I couldn't deny it any longer—I was in love with John. But a sense of sadness lingered, knowing that our time together would soon come to an end, albeit temporarily.

"You could come with me to Oregon," John suggested, his voice laced with longing. "That's where my actual pack is. I can't stay here."

I sighed softly through my nose as a heaviness settled within me. Oregon, a place unknown to me, held the allure of John's past, present, and future where his actual pack resided. However, I couldn't uproot myself so soon, not when I had only just reunited with my sister, Lissa. The bond between us needed nurturing, and I yearned for more moments to create cherished memories with my newfound family.

Regret and understanding mingled as I confessed, my voice tinged with sadness, "I can't leave. I need to spend more time with my sister. I just got her."

John nodded, his eyes shadowed with a flicker of sadness. Deep down, I could feel the weight of his longing, akin to the yearning of a wolf denied its mate. It pained me to witness his sadness, for I knew our connection was undeniable. But I needed time to fully embrace the depth of our bond and the responsibilities that came with it.

I couldn't deny the truth that I was John's mate, but I believed that our love would endure, strengthened by the passage of time and the challenges we would overcome. I hoped that he could understand the significance of my decision, even if it left him with a heavy heart.

As we stood in a poignant silence, the beauty of the lake reflected our complex emotions. The ever-changing water mirrored the ebb and flow of our connection.

"John," I spoke softly, my eyes meeting his with unwavering sincerity. "I just need some time to think. I promise we will find our way back to each other, stronger and more certain than ever."

I knew that our paths may temporarily diverge, but the depth of our connection would remain steadfast. And in that moment, as the sun dipped below the horizon, casting a warm glow over our entwined figures, I held onto the hope that our love would endure, transcending time and distance.

A single tear escaped my eye, tracing a path down my cheek. In that vulnerable moment, John turned towards me, his eyes filled with understanding and affection. Without a word, he leaned down and gently kissed my head.

At that moment, a surge of warmth enveloped me as if a magical current flowed through our connection. It was as if the universe itself aligned, stirring something deep within our hearts. Our bond grew exponentially, surpassing any doubt or uncertainty that lingered before. I could feel it with every fiber of my being—we were undeniably mates.

Driven by an overwhelming surge of emotions, I acted on instinct. I rushed towards John, my heart pounding in my chest, and pulled him into an embrace. Our lips met in a passionate kiss, as if time stood still and the world around us faded away. The magic that coursed through our connection intensified, binding us together in a profound and unbreakable union.

There was no room for doubt or hesitation in that moment of pure enchantment. Within that moment of shared breath, our souls seemed to have merged, intertwining with a fervor that defied explanation. The depth of our love became immeasurable, and the realization of our eternal bond washed over us like a tidal wave.

As we shared that extraordinary kiss, a symphony of emotions surged through us. Love, desire, and an unyielding sense of completeness flooded our beings. It was as if the universe had conspired to unite us, aligning our destinies with an extraordinary force.

When our lips finally parted, we remained locked in a profound embrace, our eyes reflecting the depth of our connection. There was no need for words, for in that magical moment, our hearts spoke volumes. We knew, without a shred of doubt, that we were meant to be together, united as mates for all eternity.

"Kara," he whispered, unwilling to let go.

"I know," I replied softly against his lips. I, too, didn't want to let go, but being the stubborn woman I was, I still refused to follow him to Oregon.

Days after John left, I was left with a painful hole in my heart. It was like being separated from oxygen. And everyone around could see my sadness.

I had a feeling John felt worse wherever he was. We didn't complete our bond, and I knew it was painful for him to be denied that as a wolf.

Vince had fully taken up his role as the alpha. Watching how he and Lissa were so in love with one another made me wish I had gone with John. Maybe I was depressed, too, because I had also denied myself to secure that bond with my mate.

The other day, Mera asked me, "When will you go to him?"

"What?" I replied, lost in my thoughts.

"Come on, Kara. You're miserable here. You need to go to him."

"I need to be with my sister."

"Your sister looks just fine hanging out with Vince. I'm sure he is making her happy, if you know what I mean," she chuckled. "I mean, with those muscles and that height, he's got to be big, right?"

I rolled my eyes.

"Kara…"

"I'm feeling insignificant, Mera," I said suddenly. "With the bad wolves taken care of, I … I no longer have a job here, and it's kind of difficult for me to accept. Maybe I'm a little attached to this place."

Mera smiled. She came closer to me and held my hand. "You are a lot of things, Kara. But insignificant? Never. You are the most relevant being that I know on this planet."

I smiled, and my heart sincerely warmed. "Aw. Thank you, Mera."

"Go to him, Kara. Figure out what life has in store for you by his side. You'll thank me later for it." She hugged me and then said teasingly, "At least get laid."

I laughed as I thought about her words. She always had a way to make me smile.

To be honest, I didn't think much about love. I never had. I was always too busy. But, when John entered my life, my heart, mind, and body were thrown into disarray. My wolf mused. She loved it and was urging me to go to him. I'd always known my going to Oregon was inevitable. My wolf and I missed John too much. I just needed a little push.

I packed my bags the next day and headed for Oregon.

I'm coming, my mate.

20

Kara

As I approached the front door, my body shook due to my anxiety being high. My hand reflexively went to my bare neck. No matter how many deep breaths I took, I was still nervous. I was taking a chance to show up here without saying anything. Would he be upset? Would his alpha? John hadn't talked much about his life in Oregon or his pack other than that this was where he was from and that his alpha had sent him to New York to oversee the takeover and alpha replacement. Now that was done, and everything was running smoothly, I felt like I could leave.

As I reached my hand to the door to knock, it opened, and a familiar face stood behind it.

"John," I said softly.

"Kara? You came." His eyes widened as if he were surprised I was standing before him.

"I did," I replied with a smile. The house was massive, and out of curiosity of what the interior looked like, I glanced over his shoulder to peer inside.

John opened the door and stepped aside. "Why don't you come in," he said with a warm smile.

With a racing heart, I walked into the house, my arm brushing his as I passed him. Energy seemed to crackle in the air as our eyes briefly met, smiles being exchanged. Just being near him again made me feel like I was floating.

If I had any doubts that we were meant to be together, they were now long gone. No other person had such a staggering effect on me. No one else haunted my thoughts and dreams like him.

However, we did have a lot to talk about.

"This way," John said as he led me to the right side of the large, open foyer with a long, red-carpeted hallway.

I followed him closely, my eyes sweeping over the walls adorned with intricate paintings and even a mirror or two. As I glanced at my reflection, I quickly tucked a loose strand of hair behind my ear, a nervous but excited shudder passing through me.

A deep sense of longing radiated from my soul, my wolf calling out to John with need. It was strong enough to make him look back at me, his eyes slightly darkening. He was also at his tipping point if he yearned for me as much as I did for him.

John turned away as we approached a closed white door at the far end of the east wing. He pushed it open to reveal his suite. It was a large room with tall windows, a large bed covered with dark red sheets, and dark wooden furniture.

I walked over a large, rectangular rug made of thick, white material, my heart pounding heavily. "Wow, this is nice."

"It's nice seeing you here," John replied as he watched me explore his suite.

I felt safe here with him, but I still needed him to answer some questions. I turned to face him, a serious expression forming on my face. "I haven't heard anything about Warwick. What happened to him?"

John crossed over to me and took my hand in his. "The Council took care of him."

"But what does that mean? Will he be let go after being punished? What if he comes back and tries to hurt Sophia? Or take her child?" I asked him.

John squeezed my hand. "The Council is basically the FBI or the CIA for all things supernatural. Punishment isn't taken lightly, trust me. You won't ever have to worry about Warwick ever again because all his crimes most likely had him sentenced to death."

I didn't let myself breathe just yet. "Do you think he committed enough crimes to be sentenced to death?"

"He broke many rules and regulations that are very important in supernatural society. We must hold ourselves even more accountable than humans do with their rules and laws," John assured me. "Warwick had a price on his head. The Council wanted him so that they could properly punish him."

I released a slow exhale, letting some of the tension fall from my shoulders. Around him, I could let down my walls. He was one of the few who could break past them. "Good. He doesn't deserve to live another day after all he's done."

John nodded before lifting my hand and pressing his lips against my knuckles. "It's over, Kara."

It still didn't feel real, but there was proof all around us that we were finally safe.

"Sophia and her daughter are doing great. Paul has stepped up and helped them a lot," I told him as a smile crossed my face. Not having to stress about her and her daughter's safety was nice. They were definitely in good hands.

"He's a good guy. He'll take care of them," John said.

"I think Paul is a good fit in more ways than one," I replied with a cheeky glint in my eyes. I had seen the warm looks Sophia and Paul passed each other when they thought no one was looking. There was a spark.

John chuckled. "Looks like everyone is finding their rightful mate."

My skin flushed and warmed as his hands settled on my waist, drawing me closer to him. My wolf stirred and yearned for him, for the bond that needed to be completed. I couldn't wait any longer. "John…"

John leaned closer and captured my lips in a passionate kiss, stealing my breath from my lungs.

I placed my hand on the back of his neck, my fingers teasing the hair on the back of his head. Our lips brushed and melded, falling into a perfect rhythm that generated so much heat between us that it felt like fire was burning within me.

"I love you, Kara," John whispered as his forehead touched mine. "I want you. Always."

My heart skipped as I gazed up into his comforting eyes. "And forever, my mate."

John grinned and picked me up by the back of my thighs, carrying me over to his large bed and setting me down on the edge of the mattress. His lips found my neck, a low growl sounding from him as he inhaled my scent.

My eyes fluttered shut as I buried my fingers in his hair, holding him close as he kissed every crevice and sensitive spot. Heat washed over me, desire pulsing between my thighs as he slotted himself between them.

John grabbed the bottom of my dress and slipped it off me, his fingers quickly undoing the clasp of my bra to let my breasts spill out. His hands and mouth were instantly on me, kneading my flesh and teasing my hardened nipples.

I threw my head back as my thighs tightened around his waist. His erection strained against his dark pants, pressing against my inner thigh dangerously close to my center. "Please… more."

John chuckled against my skin. He flicked his tongue across one of my nipples before gently grasping my chin to draw my eyes to his. "I'll give you the world."

A blissful smile appeared on my face, my wolf nearly whining at this point for him. For the mate bond. I could feel my wolf trying to take control, pressure forming under my gums as my fangs tried to break free in due time.

John sank to his knees in front of me, tearing my black panties off and nudging my thighs apart. He pressed his mouth flush against my center, his tongue drifting through my folds to seek out my sensitive nub.

"John!" I cried out as my head dropped against the mattress once he found it. I curled my fingers in his hair, waves of pleasure crashing down on me as he savored my scent and my taste. The tip of his tongue flickered across my pearl, unrelenting, causing my hips to buck in response.

"You taste incredible," John growled against my skin. He left an open-mouthed kiss against my inner thigh, and I swore I felt a light graze from a fang. He was teetering on the edge as well.

As his tongue stroked over my clit once more, he pushed a finger inside my slicken channel. I closed my eyes, my lips parting with pleased sounds. Every lick and every thrust of his finger inside of me threatened to unravel me. As good as it felt, I wanted to come with him inside me. I wanted everything.

I wanted the bond.

"I need you," I breathed out, tugging on his hair.

John detached from me with glistening lips. His eyes were hazed over with lust. They had changed from dark blue to golden, and I knew he was on the cusp of a mating frenzy. There was no turning back, not that I wanted to. No, I wanted this. I wanted my mate more than the air that I breathed.

As John tore off his clothes, he licked his lips and hummed. He grinned at me as if he was savoring my taste. His hand wrapped around his hardened cock, slowly stroking it as he crawled on the bed over me. The tip glistened as he rubbed the beads of his precum across it, adding extra lubrication. He glided through my folds and grazed over my sensitive clit.

I dug my nails into his shoulders as a moan escaped me, a pleading look filling my eyes. "John, please," I cried.

John couldn't wait any longer, either. He slowly pushed himself inside of me until he bottomed out, both of our pleased sounds mingling. He planted his forearms next to my head as he hovered over me, his lips meeting mine in a deep kiss. "I'm going to make you mine."

I nodded eagerly, nearly brought to tears with relief when he started to thrust faster into me. Every stroke was deep and hard, hitting a spot inside me that made my back arch. My nails raked up his back. "Yes, just like that."

John buried his face in my neck, kissing and teasing again, but I knew what he wanted. "So perfect. All mine."

The moment he growled those words, I felt his fangs pierce my skin, and a fire roared through me. The room fell away around us, and all I could comprehend was the pressure and burn of his bite and the intertwining of our very souls.

My sensations were his, and his sensations were mine. We were one soul, united by an indescribable bond. I could feel his deep love for me, and it was almost unbearable.

"John," I moaned, the overwhelming power and desire of my wolf finally breaking free. It was my turn. I gripped his hair and bit into his neck, making another wave of intensity and pleasure crash down on us.

John growled in bliss, snapping his hips against mine to bury himself even deeper. Our breaths grew quick and heavy, borderline panting as our blood ran hot. Our adrenaline soared. Our bodies ached with the need to keep going.

The taste of his blood flooded over my tongue, staining my lips when I pulled away with a sound of pure ecstasy. It felt like I was on fire in the most pleasurable way possible, and I could feel pressure building low in my stomach again.

John dragged his tongue over the bite mark he left, lapping up the blood trickling from the puncture wounds, his saliva sealing it. His lips hovered near my ear. "Come for me, my mate."

One more deep thrust made my entire body erupt into hard, uncontrollable shakes. My nails scratched up his back as I held onto him for dear life. My moans filled the room.

John buried himself inside of me one last time, he and his wolf roaring with pleasure. He dropped his forehead to rest against my shoulder, both of us panting to catch our breaths. After a minute, he lifted his head to gaze down at me with a warm smile. "You're incredible."

I smiled back and stroked his hair, feeling like I was floating but also tethered to him at the same time. Our mate bond was complete. Our wolves and our souls were united. "You're mine."

John leaned down and kissed my lips, sealing our intense bond with a kiss and three words.

"Always and forever."

Epilogue

John

Two Months Later

The biggest, greatest surprise of my life was meeting Kara. The moment our eyes met, I knew that there was something special about her. My wolf felt the connection immediately, and I was glad I listened.

In the midst of turmoil and danger, our love and our bond prevailed, and the last two months were a testament to that. There was so much more goodness to come.

"We have a huge thing to ask," Gemma said as she and Aiden sat on the loveseat adjacent to the leather couch Kara and I were lounging on. She shared a nervous but eager look with her mate, who kept his arm protectively and lovingly wrapped around her shoulders. She was about to pop at this point since she had twins on the way.

Kara leaned against my side as she tilted her head at Gemma. "What is it?"

Hope gleamed in Gemma's eyes as she joined her hands together pleadingly. "Will you be my midwife? You have so much experience, and there's no other person I trust to help me through the birth of my twins."

Kara's eyes widened as she sat up. She placed her hand over her heart. "Really?"

Pride beamed on my face as I rubbed Kara's back, knowing she would do a hell of a job. She was gifted and skilled in many ways and still strived to help people around here. It was in her blood.

"Absolutely. We trust you," Aiden spoke up as he shared a warm look with Gemma.

"I'd be honored," Kara said with an eager nod.

Gemma clambered to her feet, her hand holding her round stomach. When Kara stood, they threw their arms around each other in a tight embrace.

I glanced over at Aiden, who grinned at me. We were both over the moon with our mates and finally experienced peace in our lives. No more bloodshed. No more fights.

Aiden looked away when his phone started ringing. "It's Paul."

Gemma and Kara took their seats as Aiden answered.

"Hey, Paul. I'm with Gemma, Kara, and John. You're on speaker," Aiden told him.

"Hey, guys," Paul greeted us.

We all called out our greetings. Paul had been stuck across the country, ensuring the pack thrived and didn't tear each other apart. Thankfully, Vince stood by his word and ruled effectively and fairly.

"Wish you and Sofia and the baby were here!" Kara called out.

I smiled a little, hearing the longing in her voice. She missed Sofia, whom she fought valiantly for, and I knew she was very excited to see the baby. There was a lot of baby fever going on around here. Or pup fever, I supposed.

"That's actually why I'm calling. I'm coming home! And I'm bringing Sofia and her daughter with me," Paul told us.

My jaw dropped. They were finally coming home. We had all been splintered and separated for so long, and we would all finally be together soon. "That's great!"

"That's awesome. Really. If you need anything or any help getting over here, let us know," Aiden said, rubbing Gemma's arm as she beamed.

After Paul filled us in on some pack news, he hung up to spend time with Sofia and her daughter. Aiden pocketed his phone with a chuckle. "Paul and Sofia are a thing. They have to be."

The rest of us nodded in agreement. They hadn't explicitly said anything yet, but they didn't have to. It was obvious.

"Paul would make a great dad," I said. He had the patience, kindness, and protectiveness that was needed, and he already took care of Sofia's daughter like she was his own anyway.

"He would," Gemma agreed before giving us a pointed look. "Now, we're waiting for you two to contribute to the pack's future."

Aiden and Gemma laughed while Kara and I shared an amused smile. We had news of our own to share, too, and the excitement felt like it was rattling beneath my skin, dying to be let out.

"We are. Kara and I are expecting," I said, the words bursting from me as a proud grin formed across my lips.

A look of shock plastered itself on Aiden's and Gemma's faces for a few seconds before they got to their feet and dragged us into tight embraces.

"This is amazing!" Gemma gasped as she nearly squeezed the breath out of Kara, who laughed.

"We've been dying to tell you!" Kara replied.

Aiden patted me on the back. "I'm happy for you two. We were hoping it would happen soon."

"Me too. We've been really wanting this," I said before looking over at Kara, my chest aching at the sight of pure love in her eyes.

This was a whole new adventure for us. We had already gone through so much together, but this would be the most incredible journey ever. We would create a family of our own, and there was no one else I wanted to go down this road with.

Kara gravitated to me as Gemma and Aiden expressed their excitement to each other. She wrapped her arms around my neck and smiled up at me. "I couldn't ask for a better life. A better mate. I love you."

I rested my forehead against hers as my hands settled on the small of her back, pressing her closer to me. Soon, she would start showing, and things would become that much more real. I couldn't wait.

"I love you. And I love our pup on the way."

Vince and Lissa's story continues in The Rogue and the Rebel, book 3 in the Sanctuary Series. It is also available to read on Kindle Vella. The first few episodes/chapters are FREE.

Since Kindle Vella is still only available to readers in the US, it is available to everyone on Ream Stories.

An updated version of The Rogue and the Rebel will be available to read by everyone as an ebook and in paperback in September 2024.

Paul and Sophia will return in another book, as does Mason, his mate, and his hoard. As for Ciaran, he hasn't just vanished without a trace. You will see him again in a later book. You'll also learn more about the organization he works for in The Rogue and the Rebel.

About J. Raven Wilde

If you loved this story, sign up to receive J. Raven's newsletter. Subscribers get the latest information on cover reveals, new or upcoming releases, and promos. Plus, it's FREE, and she promises never to spam you or give out your information. Sign up now by clicking here. You can also follow her on her Facebook Group, Wilde Raven's Steamy Reads.

J. Raven had spent most of her life traveling around the US or abroad, managing to find a bookstore in every city she visited. She began writing as a little girl, and it slowly grew into something she loved doing.

Now that she isn't traveling as much anymore, she spends her time writing steamy romance stories at her quiet, modest home by the lake.

Printed in Great Britain
by Amazon

47415212R00099